Therian
Harbor ⚓   ★ Thera

Airport ✈

Anthinios ⚓
Harbor

Fira
Winery

Exo ◉
Gonia

Kamari ◉

Mesa
Vouno

Classical ⚒
Ruins

Akrotiri ◉

⚒ Excavation Site

Perissa
Beach

SANTORINI

SINISTER PARADISE

BECKY BOHAN

To Evie —
        Best wishes,
            Becky Bohan

Madwoman Press
1993

This is a work of fiction. Any resemblance between characters in this book and actual persons, living or dead, is coincidental.

Cover by Bonnie Liss and Pat Tong of Phoenix Graphics, Winter Haven, Florida

Edited by Diane Benison and Catherine S. Stamps

Printed in the United States on acid-free paper

Library of Congress Cataloging-in-Publication Data

Bohan, Becky, 1952–
  Sinister paradise / Becky Bohan.
     p. cm.
  ISBN 0-9630822-2-1 (alk. paper) : $9.95
  1. Women detectives—Greece—Fiction. 2. Lesbians—Greece—Fiction. I. Title.
PS3552.O488S57   1993
813'.54—dc20

                                                          93-2011
                                                          CIP

Acknowledgments

Thanks to Deb Eaton who got me started; to Ellen McEvoy for her close reading of the manuscript; to Glenda Eoyang, my business partner, for helping me realize personal goals; to each person in my Wednesday night writer's group for listening carefully, giving constructive criticism, and providing on-going support; and to Kitty Johnson for her encouragement and understanding.

To Kitty

for the adventure

About the Author

Becky Bohan was born and raised in Madelia, Minnesota. She attended the University of Minnesota in the early 70s where she was active in student and feminist politics. She received an M.A. in English Literature from the University of Wisconsin, Madison, in 1977. After working for several years in the area of computer-based education at a large corporation, she co-founded a small technical training and documentation company in Minneapolis, where she now resides.

Prologue

"The gods will drink your blood," Paulos Bountourakis spat out moments before he died.

Two hunks of hired muscle, reeking of fish and sweat, held the young photographer at the edge of the thirteen hundred foot cliffs on the island of Santorini. To his back the six–mile wide caldera yawned, its three volcanic islands glowing like phosphorous in the moonlight. Directly below him the mounds of the pumice ash mines spread their haunting shadows.

"Cut the crap, Bounty," a man said, stepping closer to the trio at the edge. "This is the last time I ask. Who do you work for?"

The fierce wind rushing across the abyss of the sea tore at the men like vultures.

"No one. This I swear on the grave of my father." The Greek's long black hair whipped painfully into his eyes and fine-boned face.

"Who knows you went to Mesa Vouno?"

Bountourakis squeezed his eyelids shut. Mesa Vouno. The granite mountain on the southeast side of the island with acres of Classical ruins on its top. He had gone only as far as the sculpted rock: the stone carvings of a lion, a dolphin, and an eagle. He set up his gear a short distance away. His camera was loaded with high-speed film and pointed at the Santorini airport in the distance. Below him, his village of Kamari had sparkled under the bright bulbs of the tavernas.

"No one."

"Not true. We knew. Lucky for us, we caught you."

"Why did you drive me here, to the other side of the island?"

"Think about it, bright boy. We don't want your body found on Mesa Vouno."

Bountourakis strained against his smelly captors. Why didn't I listen to Maria? he thought. She told me to think only of my pictures, and not to listen to men in Athens with expensive suits and causes. 'What happens if you get in trouble?' she had asked once. 'You don't know what you're doing. You are an artist, not some spy in the movies.' But I left something for you, he argued to the image of his wife. On the mountain. Between the rocks.

"A smoke, please?" the photographer asked.

"Too late." The man turned away.

The howling wind smothered Bountourakis's scream. The last pieces of the world the Greek saw as he cartwheeled through the night were hills of gray ash and the dark crater waters rushing up at him like the Furies bursting from a nightmare.

1

Britt Evans squeezed her wiry frame between the clutter of furniture in Athens's Syntagma Square and settled into a chair in front of the American Express Building. A waiter quickly appeared to take her order for an Amstel beer.

After a few sips, Britt leaned back to examine, then enjoy, the sights of the famous block. Amidst the noisy, swirling traffic, the leaves of the oak and ash trees shimmered in the warm May breeze. Water from the fountain in the middle of the square rose like a cathedral, and pockets of people gathered around small tables under green and blue canopies.

For the first time in two weeks, the Classics professor from the University of Minnesota felt free of stress. Her series of lectures at the American School, based on her book, *The Flora and Fauna of Ancient Greece*, had gone well. Now she was looking forward to an extended stay at Santorini where she would do research at the Akrotiri excavation. As she stretched in contentment, the rays of the mid-afternoon sun struck her thick, shaggy black hair, and drew a fleeting halo of navy blue on her crown.

Britt glanced at her watch. Her habitually early friend, Nicostrata Lampas, was late. She wondered if it had anything to do with the surprise Nicki said she was bringing. The women had met during Britt's graduate years at Berkeley when she was a teaching assistant for a lower division course in Greek Art. Nicki, then a senior architecture student, had been waiting outside the classroom one day for her younger brother. Soon, she was waiting for Britt with a crush as big as her bank account.

Britt surveyed the pedestrians, looking for the Greek woman. For a moment, her eyes met those of a man with a closely cropped beard leaning against a nearby lamppost. He turned indifferently to a newspaper with a slow, graceful motion.

A familiar voice called above the traffic. Nicki approached her table, looking sleek and chic. She wore gray slacks and a white linen blouse with a kerchief as black and glossy as her short hair. Tortoise-shell glasses made the young architect appear older than her twenty-six years.

"You look divine!" Nicki cried and quickly kissed Britt's cheek. The smell of a spicy perfume wafted over Britt. The petite woman stood back. "Welcome to my home," she said. A short man in his sixties appeared by her outstretched arm. Nicki clasped him fondly. "My godfather, Mikos Zerakis!"

So this was the legendary Mikos Zerakis, Britt thought, looking at the thickset man with a gold front tooth as they took their seats. From what she recalled, he was a long-time politician and current member of Parliament. He had been Nicki's advocate, persuading a reluctant father to send his only daughter to America for an education.

Zerakis, dressed in a gray linen suit that matched the shading of his hair perfectly, gave Britt a penetrating look. His eyes lingered on the slight bump on Britt's nose, the remnant of an old break, then locked onto her black, intelligent eyes. "Such a beauty!" he exclaimed. He grinned at Nicki in an approval that was not wholly affected.

"What's the issue of the day in Parliament, Mr. Zerakis?" Britt asked after the Greeks had placed their orders.

"Terrorism," he replied, frowning and shaking his head. "It is a bad situation that has no solution, no end." The godfather paused, as if unsure of whether to go on and risk boring this woman who meant so much to Nicki. But, in a moment, the politician prevailed. "Your president thinks we are too easy on terrorists. But this is the irony," he said, holding up a finger. "We open our doors to refugees, then we are blamed if a few smelly goats sneak through! Perhaps we close the American naval base next!" Zerakis slapped the table for emphasis. Britt's beer bottle rocked. "How would your president like that!"

"He'll have to speak for himself," Britt said, steadying the green bottle. "But military cutbacks may close it before you do."

Zerakis kept silent while the waiter set two glasses of wine on the table, then continued. "Those decisions are for the politicians, and this I will tell you," Zerakis smiled, "we are all a bad lot." He took a taste of the wine. "You know, we love America. She saved us in the war. Then she turned around and supported the junta and now has big money for Turkey but not for us."

"Especially after the war with Iraq," Nicki added.

"Before, the excuse was Turkey's shared border with the Soviet Union." Zerakis grunted. "Now it is to keep a foot on Iraq. There is always an excuse, yes?"

Britt poured the rest of her beer into her glass. Again she caught the stranger at the lamppost observing her. This time he folded the newspaper, tucked it under his arm, then sauntered down the street. Britt felt a flash of uneasiness at the man's interest in her, but brushed it away.

"Listen to this," Zerakis continued. "Our governments may quibble, but this is always true: The people of Greece love the people of America. Always." He raised his glass in a salute, which was returned by his two companions.

Zerakis observed Nicki's beaming face, then smiled. "But why do we go on so? The world is not all politics. There are people to love, things to see. That, too, is part of Greece." With that, Zerakis recounted the strong bloodline of Nicki's family, a clan of wealthy Corinthian landowners and businessmen.

"You leave for Santorini next Tuesday?" Nicki asked Britt. Her olive cheeks had darkened with the praise of her godfather.

"Yes. Bill and Anne, whom I'm staying with, are having a send-off party Monday night. Why don't you come? You, too, Mr. Zerakis."

"Santorini, eh?" The old Greek raised an eyebrow. "A man died there recently. A photographer at the Akrotiri excavation."

"I heard."

"Did you know him?" Zerakis asked, his eyes slicing into Britt.

"No."

"Ah," said the politician. "It is a bad business, an accident like that."

"True," Britt said, matching his gaze.

"You must be careful there. Do not tempt the fates by dancing at the edge," the government official said darkly.

"The edge of the cliffs?" Britt asked.

Zerakis pasted on the thin, knowing smile of an insider. "Yes, the edge of the cliffs." He shifted his sights to the gleaming white chapel on top of Mount Lycabettus in the distance. "Or perhaps of life."

2

After Zerakis departed for his office, Britt and Nicki made their way toward the Acropolis. They caught an occasional glimpse of its mammoth retaining walls through the thick telephone cables threaded across the sky. The blue and white Greek flag, set high above the ruins, danced on its pole.

The women spent an hour roaming around the ancient ruins. Edging their way toward the exit through a throng of tourists and misbehaving children, they paused at the western wall and looked out over the city. Directly below, where street vendors lined the pathways to the Acropolis, Britt caught sight of the strange man once more. Newspaper still in hand, he seemed more interested in the people passing by than in the articles.

"I have many projects now," Nicki said. "A small one near Sounion, a smaller one at Nauplion. A big one outside Milan where I've been for the past month."

Britt brought her attention back to her friend. "I didn't realize you were with an international firm."

"Yes. A very prestigious one. I think Mikos twisted some ears to get me hired—there is still much discrimination against women here. But it improves, a little each year."

"I'm really proud of you, Nicki," Britt said. "You're a great role model for all the women who come after you."

"Yes, I suppose." The architect adjusted her glasses. "On this project in Italy, I work on alternative housing—earth homes and solar power. I want to do the same in this country. All the Greek houses are the same here—like sugar cubes. With the right backing from the government, we will soon start experimental models in Greece. Mikos has been working hard on a funding bill."

As they descended the steep stone stairway, Britt caught
sight of the man again. This time, he stood at a public phone,
with his hand cupped around the receiver.
"Do you know that guy?" Britt asked, subtly pointing out
the man to Nicki.
"No. Should I?"
"I have a feeling he's been watching me."
"Can you blame him? I've been watching you for years."
Britt smiled weakly. She felt Nicki treading dangerously
close to old wounds. From the beginning, their friendship had
been unsettled, split between the shared joy of the classics
and the misery of unrequited attraction. On one hand, they
were united in appreciation of a temple's entablature, but on
the other, divided by Nicki's denial that Britt could prefer
another woman—or no one at all—to her. Nicki had developed an annoying habit of always reminding Britt of her
devotion.
"You are single now?"
"Yes. I plan to stay that way, Nicki." Britt turned away
from her piercing eyes, wishing to close the subject.
Rebuffed once again, Nicki acquiesced. If not now, she
hoped, perhaps another time.

Britt and Nicki travelled through the narrow, winding
streets of the old part of Athens called the Plaka, which was
filled with the aroma of cheese, cooked lamb, and sewage.
They turned onto the cobbled street of Adrianous and walked
past the lush courtyard of Saint Katherine's church. As they
entered the final block of the old city that intersected with a
major thoroughfare, Britt heard a strange rattling, then the
gunning of an engine behind them. Curious at hearing a car
in an area where vehicles were banned, Britt glanced behind

her and saw a battered Renault pickup hurtling down the street towards them.

Britt quickly took in the sight. The delivery truck's green paint had faded to olive, and the front bumper sloped in front of a dented chrome grill. Behind the wheel, a man with a *keffiyeh* wrapped around his head, gripped the steering wheel with one gloved hand. The Arab headgear covered all but his eyes, which were hidden behind wrap–around sunglasses.

The Renault's gears shifted. The wooden slats that fenced in the bed of the truck held a substantial payload of olive oil tins and mesh bags filled with oranges. The ten–liter cans toppled out of their restraining ropes and crashed onto the pile of fruit as the vehicle gained speed.

"Jump!" Britt shouted to Nicki, tugging her friend over the curb and out of the street. The driver swerved the Renault to the left. The truck's left tires thudded against the curb, then gained the sidewalk. The Renault came at the women like a listing speedboat. The side mirror snapped off as it hit a window ledge. There was nowhere to run.

The pigeons strutting along Saint Katherine's red tiled roof squawked at the commotion and flapped into the hazy sky. Tourists outside a souvenir shop across from the church spun around to find the source of the uproar.

Britt grabbed Nicki and pushed her along the sidewalk. "In here!" she cried, flattening herself and the architect into a recessed doorway four steps away. As the truck whooshed past, Britt felt the door handle brush across her nylon fanny pack.

Then it was over. The truck wheeled south around the corner by the Arch of Hadrian and disappeared. The street suddenly was quiet, with only the toots of distant traffic to be heard.

"My god," Britt said, as she stepped out from the doorway. "Are you okay?"

"Fine," Nicki said, tucking in her blouse and adjusting the silver buckle on her belt. "And you?"

Britt pointed at a dirt smudge on her fanny pack. "All considered, just fine." She swallowed hard. Her throat was as dry as felt. "What was that all about? He was trying to run us down on purpose."

"I don't know." Nicki gazed down the empty road.

"But why would someone do that?"

"Again, I have no answer." Nicki, pale and a little shaky, managed a tiny smile. "I do have the license plate number."

"Good for you!" Britt cried, giving Nicki a pat on the shoulder. "Let's give it to the police."

"No," Nicki said. "Do nothing, say nothing, for now."

"Listen, some guy almost killed us..."

"I know." The Greek's face hardened with determination. "It will be taken care of. By my godfather."

3

Monday evening Bill and Anne MacKenzie hosted a small send–off party for Britt, their houseguest. Their two–bedroom apartment, nestled in the upscale Kolonaki district and decorated with bright, Middle Eastern art and Scandinavian furniture, held a mild sprinkling of guests.

The Santorini incident threaded its disconcerting way through the evening's conversations, which focused primarily on departmental gossip and the continuing fall of the U.S. dollar. The few people who had attended the photographer's funeral reported that the Akrotiri crew was hard at work again.

Britt knew most of the people at the party, if not by name, then by sight. Judy, an art history instructor and colleague of Bill's at the American School, sat in the corner. She coolly observed Britt, sitting across from her, and tugged on a large hoop earring hanging under a sheath of bleached, spray–hardened hair. "How long will you be in Santorini?" she asked, her languid voice confirming the boredom in her expression.

Britt's eyes widened. It was the first time that Judy had ever initiated a conversation with her. "Four to five weeks," she replied.

"Good god," the instructor said, without changing her tired pitch, "two full days is enough to drive me insane, staring out at those black islands reeking of sulfur. No thank you."

"I find it has a haunting beauty," challenged Bob Collins, a graduate student in his early thirties sitting next to Judy. He ran his hand over his brown beard and leaned forward, resting his arms on his knees. His legs spread across the width of a couch section. "Actually, it's quite an interesting place if you want to poke around. Lots of good folklore, like vampire bats and ghosts, things that have been overlooked because of the excavations, and, of course, the inane theory that Santorini was once Atlantis."

"Ghosts. Now that's appropriate," Judy said, "since the place is about as close to a hell on earth as you're likely to come. Hell must suit you, though, Robert, seeing how often you visit that inferno."

Bob pointed the neck of his Beck's bottle toward Judy, then poured half of its contents down his throat. Judy clicked her tongue and stroked her mascara–laden eyelashes.

A sudden movement across the room drew Britt's attention. Just as she turned, she saw a man in his forties coming straight at her with strong, purposeful steps. Britt started slightly, unused to such displays of directed and intense energy. His dark eyes possessed a quick intelligence.

"Hello, Miss Evans. I'm Rich Marcello—an acquaintance of Bill's." He clasped Britt's hand in a firm, authoritative shake. "May I join you?"

Without waiting for a response, Marcello settled in the chair next to Britt and, in turning toward her, excluded all others from the conversation.

"Unfortunately, Bill's been too busy to introduce me," he said. Britt cast an eye toward the host who was entertaining a small knot of friends with a play–by–play of the discovery of Bountourakis's shattered body. A pink flush of excitement had spread across the art professor's scalp, visible through thinning reddish blond hair.

"I've been eager to meet you, but I couldn't make any of your lectures," Marcello continued, "so I took the liberty of asking your host for an invitation."

"My pleasure, Mr. Marcello." Britt examined the newcomer. His erect posture hadn't sagged with his sitting, and his short brown hair barely curled over the collar of his navy suit jacket. Military background, Britt guessed.

"I read your book. Interesting stuff," he said, swooping a glass of wine from a silver tray. He glanced out the glass doors that lead to a small balcony as he took a sip of wine.

Britt caught a who–is–this–buffoon glance from Bob.

"There certainly were a number of plants and animals you mentioned that aren't around today," the newcomer said in a deep, resonant voice.

"It's due primarily to deforestation," Britt explained, flipping her hair over the collar of her red silk blouse. "Crete, for instance, used to be covered with cedar forests. But over the centuries, the trees were cut. The animals were either hunted to extinction or died due to loss of their natural habitat."

Marcello cleared his throat. "Would you mind if we continued this conversation outside? I'm not used to having the air conditioning set at frigid."

"I'd like that. It is chilly in here." Britt glanced at Bob and Judy across the way who sat quietly, straining to hear her conversation with Marcello.

Marcello rose without joggling the wine in his glass. He undid the sticky latch as easily as blinking, then slid the door aside. Like a traffic cop, he crooked an arm to motion Britt along. Marcello shut the door firmly behind them.

Although the balcony held a small, round table and two white plastic chairs, Britt stayed on her feet, as did Marcello, who set his glass down, then leaned on the marble balustrade. "After what happened with deforestation, you'd think the government would jump on the environmental bandwagon."

"Well, the environment ministry is finally getting serious about reducing the sulfuric acid dissolving the national monuments and the *nefos*—that brown cloud of pollution that's eating our lungs even as we speak. As far as I know, though, Greece doesn't have any coherent land– or water–use policies to speak of, which is a shame." A small frown tugged Britt's mouth. "I hope they don't wait until their natural resources are as eroded as their temples."

"How about appealing to the government to take better care of the country?"

"It's never crossed my mind, Mr. Marcello. I'm a scholar, I'm afraid, not a politician."

"Oh? I would think that Mikos Zerakis would lend a friendly ear."

"Mikos Zerakis," Britt repeated, suddenly feeling that the appearance of this man, and his leading her to the privacy of the balcony, had been guided by a secret agenda.

"I understand that you know him."

"How on earth do you know that?" Britt demanded, then spotted her host through the windows. "Oh, Bill must have mentioned it."

"Something like that." Marcello leaned forward and lightly touched her forearm. "Forgive me, Britt. I didn't mean to alarm you."

Britt withdrew her arm. "I'm annoyed, not alarmed. When it comes to privacy, the American community here is like a small town."

An easy, vibrant laugh escaped Marcello.

"If you want to know something about me," she said, "ask me up front." Her firmly set mouth drew her strong cheekbones into tight angles.

"Fair enough." Marcello folded his arms across his broad chest and settled back against the balcony railing. "Tell me, then, how do you know Zerakis?"

"First tell me who you are and what you want. I have a feeling you're here for purposes other than reader appreciation."

"Expecting reciprocity, eh?" Marcello said, with a slanted smiled. "I work for the U.S. Embassy."

"Are you a diplomat?"

The partial smile bloomed into a full one, showing a mouth full of straight, even teeth. "I'm afraid not. Call me a bureaucrat of the State Department."

"Is your job title 'Bureaucrat,' or do you have one that's a little more descriptive?"

"I'm a Senior Foreign Service Officer. I directly assist the Ambassador."

"How do you assist him?"

"Quite well, if my promotions are any indication," Marcello said, giving Britt a hundred watt smile now. "Actually, my specialty is in government policy. For the past three months, I've been working on some environmental policies, none of which I'm free to discuss right now. But, as you might imagine, I found your study relevant."

"Really? In what way?"

Marcello lifted the glass slowly to his mouth and barely wet his lips. "Mainly by showing me how much this country has lost. When my tour is up, I'm thinking of transferring to Interior. I can use what I'm learning now to help stop the extermination of species in the States."

"That sounds very noble."

"I don't mean it to be." Marcello took another sip of wine. "Enough about me. Tell me how you came to write your book."

Britt told the embassy official of how the idea had come to her while writing her dissertation when she could find so little data about plant and animal life during ancient times. Then she went into a short history of her doctoral studies at the University of California.

As Britt wound up her story, a gentle knock rattled the doors. Bob Collins stood on the other side of the glass with a carafe of wine hoisted aloft. Britt slid open the door,

wondering how long the grad student had been standing
there. Both she and Marcello held out their glasses for refills.
After Bob had closed the door and retreated, Marcello
settled against the railing once again. "Now, tell me more
about Zerakis."
"Why do you want to know about him?"
"Call it perverse curiosity."
Britt shook back her tangle of hair and breathed in the
evening air. It had just a touch of coolness. "I met Zerakis
last Friday for the first time. He's the godfather of a college
friend."
"Godfather?" Marcello chuckled sarcastically. "Mr. Z is
godfather to half the population. It's the only way the old goat
can get elected. The loyalty of five million godchildren is
better than a vault full of PAC money." Tiny muscles on
Marcello's face played tug of war for a moment. "No, I
shouldn't diminish the guy. He's a populist. The Greeks love
him like he's some folk hero. He must spend a small fortune
on Christening gifts, though."
"Maybe he buys wholesale."
"Or has a Toys–R–Us franchise. Which godchild of his
do you know?"
"Nicostrata Lampas," Britt said before she had time to
think otherwise.
Marcello shook his head. "The name's not familiar."
"You can meet her if you like. She should be stopping by
later tonight."
Marcello glanced at his watch. "How much later?"
"Within an hour."
"Can't stay that long. I'm pressed for time as it is."
"Tell me, what's wrong with my meeting the godfather of
an old friend?"
"Nothing, if you like a beehive with a very cranky queen.
Zerakis's loyalists scurry all over town like a thousand Baker

Street Irregulars. They'll untie every bundle of laundry to scrape up the tiniest detail about anybody they choose."

"You mean he's into extortion?" She pictured the gray-haired man she had met recently. He was a powerful, arrogant, somewhat coarse man, but a crime king? Britt couldn't believe it.

"Not in the conventional sense. As far as I know, he doesn't squeeze people for money." Marcello rolled the wine glass between his palms and studied the motions of the Chablis. "But that's his genius. The nobodies he chums up with somehow blossom into somebodies after five, ten years. You know, middle-managers, bankers, shippers, corporate VPs—people who can feed him a steady stream of information. He's like a baseball scout, always looking for the potential ace who can shut down the game in the ninth."

"He sounds like the consummate politician."

"You could say that. He's a power jockey, that's for sure. He has friends everywhere at every level of society, he knows everything, and he's as judgmental as hell."

"Sounds like you've tangled with him."

"Not personally. He's end-run some of my colleagues, though. A guy on our staff had his marriage bust up and his career nearly ruined. His wife conveniently found out he had a Greek mistress—a goddaughter, no doubt—thanks to one of Mr. Z's lackeys." Marcello slid his eyes toward Britt. "Not that I approve of that sort of stuff. Anyway, just be careful of the guy."

"Don't worry," Britt said, finishing the last of her wine. "I don't trust Greek men much."

"What about American men?"

"I'm a little better, there. But just a little." She set her glass on the table.

"For some reason, I'm not surprised," he said, his eyes brightening. "Listen, Britt, I've stayed longer than I should.

I'd like to see you again. What time does your plane leave tomorrow?"

"Nine–thirty."

"How about if I pick you up at seven and take you to breakfast at the embassy? I'll have you to the airport in plenty of time."

"Why?" Britt locked eyes with Marcello.

"I have some information about Santorini that you might find interesting—it could affect your stay. I don't want to discuss it here, though."

Britt studied Marcello for a moment. "I've made arrangements for a ride to the airport, but I'll see what I can do."

"I'll give you my card," he said, reaching into his front pocket. Holding the card in his palm, he scribbled on the back. "My home phone," he explained as he held it out. "Until tomorrow morning?"

"I'll plan to see you then," Britt said, pocketing the card, "but don't bother to pick me up. I'll meet you at the embassy at seven."

From the balcony Britt watched Marcello walk briskly down the street, the heels of his polished shoes clicking sharply against the pavement.

"You're still here. Is everything okay?" Bob stood in the doorway, trapping Britt on the balcony. "I hope I'm not disturbing you."

"I'm fine, thanks. I just needed some fresh air."

"Oh, good." Bob toed one of the chairs with a scuffed Reebok hightop, its tongue running up his shin and the shoestrings trailing to the floor. "I have to get going, too." He paused, then edged his eyes up to meet the professor's gaze. "I've been waiting all evening to get you alone. I have an enormous favor to ask, Britt." His brown eyes were bright with excitement, and a little fear.

"Yes?"

"Since you're going down to Santorini tomorrow, I thought maybe you'd take a letter to a friend of mine. She's at the excavation. It would beat the mail."

"Just a letter?"

"That's all."

Britt could tell it wasn't all, not nearly. Passion was involved, passion troubled by something. Separation, perhaps. Or rejection. Britt fingered the envelope. It was white with the name "Cassie Burkhardt" scrawled in big, loose letters across the front and underlined.

"Sure," she said, cutting past Bob and making her way into the living room. "I'll deliver it."

Bob sighed with more sadness than relief. "Thanks a million."

As Britt looped through the guests on her way to the kitchen, she caught Bill by the sleeve and pulled him aside. "Why didn't you tell me about your friend Richard Marcello from the embassy?"

Bill's golden eyebrows jumped toward his receding hairline. "Marcello?" he said, chomping an ice cube. "Never heard of the guy."

4

Richard Marcello settled his clean–shaven chin on his fists and pondered the closed Santorini folder. It defied him, glaring from the center of his mahogany desk like the Saigon informants he had bought long ago. The price was cheap, but was the intelligence worth it? A softly closing door down the hall broke the stillness of his darkened office. Only low–intensity lights above two Remington wild west prints provided illumination. A faint knock sounded, followed by a deep voice saying, "Praying or thinking?"

The furrows on Marcello's brow evaporated as he broke into a boyish grin. "Neither."

Alexander Stamos swung into a straight–backed chair directly across from the embassy official. "How did it go, big man?" He spoke with a thick Greek accent.

"I've enchanted her," Marcello said, reaching for his narrow red tie coiled in his oak in–basket. "I had to spend half the goddamn evening yakking about pollution and endangered species to do it."

Stamos roared. "A tree lover, eh?"

"I expected as much. See my tongue," Marcello said, dropping his jaw for a quick show. "I had to bite half of it off."

"Your mood is splendid tonight," Stamos said. He knew his friend ranted at times without meaning half of what he said.

Marcello launched his tie toward a small American flag implanted in a chunk of walnut. "Ringer!" he cried as the silk strip caught the thin pole and its flying ends dropped over the front edge of the desk.

Stamos fished a packet of Cleopatras from his jacket and shook out a cigarette. He snapped his lighter several times before a flame held. "You read the report again, eh?" he asked, eyes on the manila rectangle.

"Yeah," Marcello said, suddenly tired. He rubbed his face with his palms. "I agree with you, Alex. Santorini could use a check. We don't have a clue as to what Bountourakis was busting his chops on. What a stupid, worthless message he sent you: 'Something happening here. Will check it out.'"

"One of the many problems in dealing with amateurs. They substitute melodrama for thoroughness."

"No argument here."

"His death certainly was convenient for someone."

"You say. I'm not totally convinced."

Stamos waved his cigarette in a dismissive gesture. "You know me...always the pessimist." He took a long drag, closing his eyes to the familiar pleasure of smoke filling his lungs. The law officer ran a hand over his dark, greased–back hair. His yellow shirt, open at the collar, revealed tufts of chest hair. Although only in his middle forties, Stamos had a face that seemed to carry the imprint of half a dozen tire treads. Too much smoke, sun, and worry.

Marcello picked at the corner of the folder, but didn't open it. "All right. We've beaten every angle possible. Your people are stretched to the limit with airport bombings and hijackings. Your art theft investigations are limited to the glamour rip–offs."

"Bah!" Stamos sucked on his cigarette. "It is Van Gogh or who cares? Even Interpol is a dry teat these days. Personally, if some fool wants to stuff a few Minoan crocks in his shorts, take them, I say. Unless, of course, they are full of poppy powder. Then you have my interest, you see."

"Yes, from the moment you suggested our finding another stooge."

"If you can set up this girl on Santorini, we will know what's happening without the commitment of funds or internal resources. That, Richard, is pure efficiency."

"And cunning. We don't have to rouse the official investigators from their full-time siesta. While they're curled up with their pillows or mistresses, we can kick over some rocks. Who knows, maybe we'll find a crooked little island gendarme under one."

"It is the best we can do. We have no covert capabilities," Stamos said. "Christ, Santorini is less than thirty square kilometers. One stranger mixing with the locals at this time, asking questions..." He drew a finger across his throat. "These people—if there are such people—are not stupid."

"The official police report could just as well have been written in crayon," Marcello complained. "It's so amateurish we can't begin to guess what really went down that night. So, we're left with Britt Evans." The American drummed his fingers on the folder. "The one person with a perfect—and legitimate—reason for being on the island, for poking into smelly corners, and eyeballing the dirt dusters at the archaeological site."

Stamos blew a smoke ring. "She is perfect." He watched the circle expand like a nebula.

Marcello stared out the window. The murky gray night sky reflected back the lights of the city. A timid whir sounded from the ventilation system.

"What if she ends up like Bountourakis?" Stamos asked.

"Then we'd know there's gas in the mine."

"What do you mean?"

"If our second canary dies," Marcello explained, "then the first didn't topple off his perch by accident. It would be proof positive of criminal activity on Santorini."

The Greek launched another squiggle of smoke. "My god, you have a hard heart."

"I didn't mean to sound that way. Listen, I like the girl. Nothing will happen to her, if I can help it."

Stamos shook out another cigarette. After lighting it, he examined his friend carefully. They had met four years ago when Marcello came to Athens, stepping confidently into a big promotion. Liaison to the Greek Criminal Investigative Services was only one of his many tasks. He was bright, a clear thinker. They had liked each other immediately. That didn't stop him from being a spear–length pain in the ass at times.

"You will tell her there may be danger?"

"I'll be candid."

"If she says no to your proposition, she will keep quiet?" Stamos's thick eyebrows squeezed together over a long, thin nose.

"You saw the report on her. Integrity seems to be her middle name."

"And the Zerakis connection?"

"A coincidence. He's the godfather of an old college friend. She met him for the first time the other day. If there were more to it, she wouldn't have blabbed to some of her colleagues at the school about meeting him."

Stamos snorted as he crushed his cigarette in a marble ashtray. "I wonder if anything concerning Mr. Z would qualify as a coincidence. Perhaps Zerakis has already re-cruited her to be one of *his* informants."

Marcello shook his head. "No chance. Her connection is strictly personal."

"So they all are, at the beginning."

"This time, I'm in the game."

"Do not be over confident," Stamos warned.

"I'm not. I know that I don't have the usual screws to turn," Marcello said. "She doesn't receive any government grants

we could threaten to cut off, and I understand she wouldn't
be interested in my charms."

"Your wife will be happy to hear that. Perhaps you have
a more challenging sales job than you led me to believe."

"On the contrary," Marcello said, stealing a grin from the
Cheshire cat. "With scholars, their passion can be both their
greatest strength *and* their greatest weakness."

5

"The truck was stolen from a merchant in Omonia Square," Nicki reported when she had Britt alone. The William Tell Overture galloped through the MacKenzie apartment, Bill's cue to his company that the party should end. A dozen hangers–on paid no attention.

"Lucky for him that he reported it stolen before it was used to run us down."

"Damn," Britt said, setting her glass on a book shelf. A small circle of wine sloshed from side to side.

"The *keffiyeh* was probably stolen, too. Police found it in the truck—it had been abandoned by the Olympic Stadium."

"What does your godfather think about this incident."

Nicki shrugged. "He says Greece is a land of mysteries. We did talk to the police."

"Their response?"

"They said people are careless behind the wheel, especially when they drive a stolen vehicle. I'm sorry we could not do more." Tchaikovsky's music jumped a couple of decibels. Nicki smiled knowingly at Britt. "Listen, I should go."

"We didn't have much time together. I'll walk you to your car."

"I had to park several blocks away."

"Good." Britt tracked down Anne MacKenzie, who was rinsing glasses in the kitchen sink, to tell her she was stepping outside for a few minutes.

"Are you still living with your brothers?" Britt asked as she and Nicki slowly stepped down the curved marble stairway to the ground floor.

"Only two. The baby moved back to Corinth to be with Mama. Papa is teaching him to be a lord of land and commerce, along with the others."

"Is Mikos Zerakis a godfather to your brothers, too?"

"Yes. All six."

"Is he a relative?"

"Not by blood, but my father and he are like fingers on a hand. Very close."

The lobby, not a direct recipient of air–conditioning, felt stuffy. The withered concierge, petrified behind a marble–topped counter, deepened her frown as the Greek and American passed.

Britt shoved open the large glass doors against the heavy Athens air. "You lead the way," she said.

As they walked toward the church across the way, Nicki folded Britt's elbow in her hand. She savored the electrical charge that bolted through her limbs at the touch and wondered how it was possible that Britt could feel nothing.

"Now, then," the professor said. "Mikos and your family."

Nicki waited as a bakery van rumbled by. "Mikos and my father fought together in the resistance during the war. When the British blocked their food supplies in '44, they almost starved to death in the mountains."

"The British?" Britt said, stepping over a soft swirl of dog excrement. "But the resistance fought the Germans."

"Ah, but the Communists led the resistance. The British believed that the more Communists who died in the war, the less they'd have to face during reconstruction."

"Did it work?"

"Partially. Thousands died and the monarchy was restored after the war, but like everything, it was temporary."

They angled down a street leading toward Syntagma Square.

"You sound bitter."

"Then you are hearing the voice of my father. To me, it's ancient history."

"And Mikos?"

Nicki adjusted her glasses. "Bitterness does not suit a politician."

Their footsteps echoed loudly on the dark sidewalk. On a balcony above them, an elderly couple sipped drinks from tall glasses as they took in the night sounds of the quiet neighborhood.

"So, are you meeting any women? Making friends? I got the impression from your last letters that you've been busy— and isolated."

"Mostly true. I belong to a feminist group, and one of the men's bars has a women's night. But that is all. It is hard for us here. You are so lucky in America." Nicki stopped in front of a baby blue Cressida GT. "Are we still on for breakfast?"

"I'm sorry, I can't make it," Britt said as the Greek thumbed through a ring of keys. "Something's come up. Maybe when I come back in a few weeks for the symposium."

Nicki turned from her disappointment as she unlocked the car door. "Get in. I'll give you a ride back."

"Thanks. I'd rather walk."

Nicki climbed into the car and rolled down the window. "You are too independent."

"We all are. Consider it a strength, not a flaw," Britt said. She leaned down to peck the young woman on the cheek. Instead, Nicki turned her face toward Britt and caught her full on the mouth.

"Lampas, you're as incorrigible as ever," Britt said.

"Just lonely."

Britt felt her reserve melt. She kissed her again, soft and steady, tasting the Retsina that Nicki had been drinking. When she pulled back, she brushed Nicki's bangs to the side.

"Maybe you should move back to America. I'll help you get a green card and find a job."

"I think about it sometimes."

"Nicki, I want you to find someone and fall so hard in love..."

"That I forget about you? That would be nice." Nicki showed a row of perfect teeth. "I know, Britt, that you are not my destiny. But I still like your kisses."

Britt laughed and gave her a final quick kiss. Although she waved cheerfully as Nicki squealed away from the curb, when she headed back toward the MacKenzies, she felt a sudden stab of loneliness herself. I'm okay, she told herself. But as she passed a jewelry store, its brightly lit window lined with gold rings and bracelets, she felt a lump rising to the top of her throat. What wonderful gifts, she thought, but I have no one special in my life to give them to.

She fixated on a gold and lapis necklace as self–doubts rose. I've been single for two years now. Is that too long? Will I ever find anyone? What is *my* destiny? Britt stared at her reflection. Her relationship with Cynthia had lasted a year. The last one, with Wendy, only six months. They, and the few others before them, had left her in tears and confusion. What wasn't working? she asked herself. Why do I keep blowing it? Why can't I pick the right person for once?

Britt had not been smart in love, she could admit that to herself now. Her friends had seen it all along. She remembered their gentle warnings. Be careful. Take things slowly. We don't want to see you hurt. But her heart, her choices, had taken her down that agonizing slope of unequal love too many times.

Really, though, she argued with herself, being single for so long had been the best thing to happen to her. She had become self–reliant — perhaps even a bit remote. She prided herself in being able to admire another woman's attractive-

ness on an intellectual level, but feel no desire. On those rare
occasions when she did sense a flint striking her heart, she
had been able to create such a lengthy catalog of drawbacks
to the attraction that no spark had a chance to ignite. Now
that, she smiled to herself, was the power of the rational mind
to bully the heart's emotion.

Britt moved on up the street and again turned her attention
to the outside world. As she passed a colorfully lit kiosk, the
headline of the *Herald Tribune* caught her attention: U.S.
Sailors Injured in Piraeus Bar Fight. More fuel for Mikos
Zerakis's antagonism toward America, she thought. On impulse, she whirled around to read the opening paragraph of
the story. A man a short distance behind her froze suddenly
at the unexpected move, but Britt saw him. The cropped
beard, the close–set eyes, and the smirking twist of his mouth
were familiar. He was the same one who had followed her
from Syntagma Square to the Acropolis.

Well, old friend, Britt said to herself, it's time we met. She
bolted into the street toward him, tacking around the rear of
a passing Mercedes and squeezing between two parked cars.

The dark figure broke into a gallop, weaving in and out of
a smattering of pedestrians like a running back. Britt mim-
icked his twists and turns, but with every step lost ground to
the thin shadow. The odor of tar and car fumes nauseated
Britt as her breathing deepened.

"Wait!" she called out. "Wait! I want to talk!"

But the man pressed on. The gap widened to thirty yards.
Suddenly his steps shortened.

He's slowing, Britt thought. I've got him.

Just then, the stranger whipped around a corner leading
into an alley. When Britt reached the narrow opening, the
dim, dirty lane seemed deserted. Britt edged quietly along the
brick building for a few feet, then stopped.

Against the blare of horns and rumble of engines in the distance, the alley vibrated with a dangerous silence. Britt inched forward, eyes on three trash cans at the dead end of the alley. They provided the only hiding place. A discarded newspaper lifted in the night breeze, then settled on the pavement.

As Britt cautiously stepped ahead, she slightly curled the ends of her fingers, forming the straight outer edge she'd learned years ago in a self–defense class. She wished she hadn't had the last glass of wine.

She consciously breathed in the putrid smells of urine and rotting food so she'd have air to scream for help if needed. Still no movement, no sounds except the distant traffic and the strains of bouzouki music floating down from an apartment overhead.

Halfway down the alley, Britt stopped to consider the wisdom of her creeping along a dark alley, each step bringing her closer to possible harm. Suddenly, behind her, a door swung open. Britt spun around. A backlit figure filled the frame, then stepped into the alley to face the professor.

Britt locked on his face, the right side aglow from light streaming out the open door. He was an old man with a grizzled gray beard. A flurry of Greek exploded from him.

Shaking her head, Britt pointed toward the end of the alley. "I look for my dog," she said, about three times louder than her normal speaking voice. She ventured half a dozen variations of what she thought would pass for 'dog' in modern Greek.

The old man seemed to understand, but he turned his head slowly from side to side. He lifted a broad, twisted hand in the direction of the trash cans, then made a motion to the left. Britt, glad for the witness, continued down the alley under the scrutiny of the old Greek. When she reached the row of garbage cans, she knew what he had been trying to communicate. The alley was not a dead end. A three–foot wide opening appeared on the left side, leading behind the brick structure and on to a maze of small paths connecting the apartment buildings in the area.

"American," the old man said, as Britt made her way back to the street. She nodded at him and noted the look of disdain in his eyes. He knew she was lying. He had probably heard someone tear down the alley and had come out to catch the excitement.

Flushed with adrenalin and embarrassment, Britt regained the city street and turned for the MacKenzie apartment. Her steps echoing on the pavement, she fingered the small, stiff card in her pocket.

Something's going on, she thought, and I'll bet every academic degree I have that Rich Marcello is behind it.

Britt yanked out his business card for a closer look. Yes, it said the U.S. Embassy. She'd be there tomorrow morning, and by god, she was going to get some answers.

6

The oak door of Rich Marcello's office made a small pop as the security guard pulled it closed behind him. Britt had only a moment to notice the beige walls and furniture, the cowboy prints, and the almost total absence of knickknacks. A romantic without sentiment? Was that possible? she thought.

"Party last long?" Marcello asked. As Britt settled on a corner sofa, he mentally reviewed his strategy of persuasion.

"Long enough." Britt passed a hand across her eyes. The olive tone of her skin seemed vaguely bleached. "I need three more hours of sleep to feel human."

"How about some caffeine to punch you up?" Marcello nodded to a silver service of coffee and a plate of rolls on a kidney-shaped coffee table.

"Please. Make it black."

Marcello eased his athletic frame into a chair next to Britt. He poured a hot stream into a cup, then held out the china with a steady hand.

"You know, Rich," Britt said after a fortifying swallow, "I don't know what to make of you, and I suspect that pleases you."

Marcello poured a second cup of coffee for himself and let his guest continue.

"Why all the lies?"

"Lies?" Marcello echoed. He noted that Britt had taken the offensive, and he was pleasantly challenged by it.

"You lied about knowing Bill. He'd never heard of you. You lied about reading my book. As a teacher, my b.s. antennae are pretty sensitive. Why?"

As Marcello mentally repositioned a few blocks of his strategy, he held out a silver tray with rolls on it. Britt plucked up a cheese–filled pastry and centered it on a small plate. "Because you're a civilian," Marcello said, returning the server to the table. "If Uncle Sam signed your paychecks and you had a security clearance, I wouldn't have wasted my time with the bullshit. Then I could have yanked you into my office and given you an assignment. As it stands, I've had to run a security check on you, have one of my men chat up some folks over at the American School, and finally scope you out personally."

"And in the process, lose my trust of you."

"I'm not so transparent to all people. It's part of the odds. I came out a few animals short of a zoo on this one. Another time I won't."

Britt bit off a small piece of her roll and chewed slowly. "What do you want of me?"

"It has to do with Santorini." Marcello tore off a chunk of doughnut and popped it into his mouth.

"I'm listening."

"Nuh–uh," Marcello said, chewing vigorously, "not so fast. I need a promise from you. You have to trust me and I have to trust you."

Britt studied Marcello for a moment. His eyes were as clear and sharp as they had been the night before. How could she tell when he was lying? "I can't trust you, Rich, at least not yet, but that doesn't mean I'll betray you. I'll hold everything you say in confidence."

"You are an honest son–of–a–gun, aren't you?" Marcello leaned toward the professor, his eyes darkening with intensity. He sensed her nibbling at the hook. "This information is to be held airtight, okay? No leaks."

"You have my word."

"Good." Marcello wet his lips, relishing a pause that seemed subtle, yet dramatic. "You said last night that you liked things up front and honest. Well, I may have screwed things up a bit, but the only way I can tell this to you is to lay it in a row. It concerns Paulos Bountourakis—the man who recently died in Santorini. You've heard of him, I assume."

"Yes. I never knew him, though."

"Bounty played Dumbo in the art circles of Europe, flitting around with his big ears wherever the creative types gathered. If he picked up bits about possible theft rings or other illegal activity, he'd zip them to his contact in the Criminal Investigative Services here in Athens, which is tied into Interpol. In five years, he had three drops. All duds."

Marcello ate another piece of doughnut then continued. "A couple of weeks ago, his contact—Alex—got a message from him on Santorini, saying he was checking out something. Before he could report, he took the Big Step over the edge."

"Was he murdered?" Britt asked, surprised at how easily the question popped out.

"I think it was an accident, as do most others. The cliffs on Santorini are a bitch. The strong winds could blow a puff like Bounty half way to Gibraltar. Believe me, if I thought he was on to something, I'd never ask a civilian to get involved." Marcello's eyes held Britt's.

"I'm still listening."

"Now comes the problem. My friend at C.I.S. isn't willing to close the file on Bounty's tip. With the guy gone, though, there's no easy way for him to find out what's happening on the island, if anything."

"Why not?"

Marcello explained the problems of resources and logistics that he and Alex had laid out the night before.

"Essentially," Marcello concluded, "what we want, is your help. If you observe anything suspicious, I want to know. I'd pass the word to C.I.S, who would then initiate an official investigation. Your work would be done once they could reopen the case."

"You want me to look for suspicious things? Like what?"

Marcello yanked the hook. "Like missing artifacts at the excavation site or museum." The government official marvelled at the elegance of the supposition. No one knew what Bounty had suspected. The smuggling of antiquities would probably be the only thing the professor would care about.

Britt rose and crossed the sea blue carpet to the window. Across the street, bright begonias hung in clay pots on stacks of apartment balconies. "I'm not comfortable with that," she said. "I'm a scholar, not some spy."

"We're not asking you to be CIA. We just want you to keep your eyelids up and tell us what you see."

"I don't know what to look for, and I don't want to go around suspecting everyone I meet. I'm out of my league, Rich. I'm..."

"That's crap and you know it. You're observant and resourceful. That puts you ahead of ninety–five percent of the population."

Britt slowly shook her head. "I appreciate your confidence in me—"

"At worst, all I'm asking is for you to help flush out a thief among your peers, if there is one."

"But why report it to you? I've known Dr. Gavas, the director of the excavation, for years. I'd tell him first."

"What if the fingerprints on the stolen artifacts belong to Gavas himself?"

"That's absurd."

"You mean you'd rather look the other way than finger a corrupt colleague?" Marcello's intense eyes followed Britt from the window back to the couch.

"Look, I don't need—I don't want—my life complicated," Britt said, resuming her seat.

"I thought you loved the world of antiquities. Won't you try to protect it?"

"Love is an individual matter. We all have different ways of expressing it. Going undercover against my own colleagues is not the way I choose to show my passion for my field."

Marcello rubbed his eyes, then blinked hard at Britt. His voice dropped. "I have no bargaining chip then. Only a plea for help. We need eyes on Santorini."

"I'm sorry. I can't—I won't—be those eyes, Rich."

"That's not what I wanted to hear." Marcello picked up the last of his doughnut.

Britt watched him chew thoughtfully, but she felt that he was really circling her, trying to find a weakness he could exploit. "It's all a game to you, isn't it?"

"It's a serious one, Britt. I've hoisted the coffins of too many friends up the cathedral steps to think otherwise."

Britt's lips parted in surprise, then closed. "That's not bull, is it?"

"No," Marcello said, the creases in his forehead deepening.

"I have the feeling that the Foreign Service isn't your only employer, that maybe..."

"No, you don't," Marcello said. "You're not interviewing me."

"At least tell me," she said, "how you fit into all this."

Marcello scanned Britt's face. The intelligence and sincerity in it softened him slightly. "One of my assignments here at the embassy is to be a link to the Greek national law enforcement agencies. One of them asked me if I knew anyone who could provide them with a quick look–see after Bounty checked out. Your name floated to the surface."

"How did that happen?"

"You registered your stay here when you first arrived, remember?"

"Ah, yes," Britt said with a nod. "Including a forwarding address to Santorini, I believe."

"Right. It was simply a matter of contacting the school for a little background information. Believe me, they think you're ready for ascension."

Britt held out her cup for a partial refill, then took a final sip. Electrons seemed to be racing from her inner ear to her toes. It was either the caffeine or the titillation of intrigue, and she decided it was time to stop which ever one it was. "How did you wind up in the State Department, Rich?"

"Via a detour called Vietnam. Two tours, actually. I got into the intelligence end of the war, enjoyed it, then finished college in the States. From there, it was just a few steps to the Foreign Service and to Athens." Rich took another hit of caffeine. "How did a Wisconsin farm girl wind up in a Classical Studies Department?"

"Ah," Britt said, her face lighting with pleasure. "Blame it on my tenth–grade teacher, the blue–haired Miss Myers. She assigned us *The Odyssey* and I was hooked for life." The professor glanced at a row of wall clocks. "It's getting late, Rich. We'd better head for the airport."

"Where's your luggage?"

"Downstairs, behind the front desk."

"Good. Let's go."

They left the embassy by a side door adjacent to the west parking lot. Marcello opened the door of his silver Saab for Britt. The interior, already broiling in the early morning sun, smelled of leather. Marcello switched on the air conditioning.

As they merged with the traffic on Kalirois, a main thoroughfare looping south past the Acropolis, Britt gave the ruins a long, regretful look. "I always find it hard to say good–bye to the Parthenon. It's a bit like leaving home."

"You have a soft spot for Athena?"

"I do."

"The Virgin Goddess. The Warrior." Marcello slid his eyes toward Britt. "What's the appeal?"

"She's also the Goddess of Wisdom."

"Hmmm." Marcello eased the car into the next lane.

Britt watched the city streets fly by. Large apartment buildings with wash strung on lines cluttered the landscape. An occasional palm or mulberry tree poked through a sidewalk, a lonely reminder of the natural world that lay beneath the concrete spread over what had once been the Argive plain.

"I have one more score to settle with you," Britt said, adjusting her seatbelt. "Who's been following me through the streets of Athens? Is he your man?"

The Saab decelerated slightly.

"What man?"

"After you left the party last night, I walked Nicki—she's Zerakis's goddaughter, remember?—back to her car. I caught someone following me, someone I'd seen before in Syntagma Square and at the Acropolis. That was the same day someone tried to run Nicki and me down in the Plaka."

"Whoa. Tell me all." Marcello listened closely as Britt recounted the episodes concerning the truck and the man in the alley. "Do you think they're connected?"

"I don't think so. The man who tried to run us down certainly wasn't the one who's been following me. He doesn't seem interested in hurting me—he had his chance in the alley."

"The tail is probably Zerakis's guy," Marcello said after a moment of deliberation. "He wants to see who his godchild hangs around with. Zerakis has pinched off more than one bud before it could blossom into scandal. He wouldn't hurt you, though. If he thought Nicki's seeing you might be an embarrassment, he'd probably pack her off to Britain or Japan for a month or two. I wouldn't worry about it. The attempted run-down, though...that one's a tough nut. Let me know if Z's people get any more information. I'll check things out through my channels, too."

Marcello guided the vehicle into the parking lot of the domestic airport. After the baggage was checked, he escorted Britt to the departure door. Leaning close, he whispered, "I hope you'll help us out. You'd have the satisfaction of breaking some sticky fingers. You have my number. Call me if you need anything."

"Maybe."

Marcello watched Britt run up the stairs into the belly of the plane. Then he whistled a few tuneless bars of celebration as he marked the turning of another citizen into an intelligence source. Britt Evans would help him. Someone on Santorini stealing artifacts? Maybe, maybe not. No matter her protests, the hook was in, and the professor wouldn't be able to shake herself free.

Thinking again of the close call with the truck, Marcello ended his self–congratulation. If the incident had indeed been an attempt to hurt Britt, why? Could someone be nervous enough about her going to Santorini that they wanted to take her out? If that were the case, they would probably try again. On the up side, they might reveal themselves, providing the opportunity for capture. On the down side, Britt Evans could lose her life.

7

As the four–engine prop plane dipped into its descent for a landing, Britt pressed her face to the window. The island of Santorini appeared below shaped like a croissant, its ends bending to the west. Steep cliffs loomed on the inside edge, remnants of the volcanic mountain that had exploded three millennia ago, sweeping away the entire Minoan civilization. Now black lava islands were growing like melanoma within the vast circle of water partially ringed by cliffs.

The plane banked to the right, bringing into clear view the pumice ash mines where Bountourakis had fallen. What a ghastly place to die, Britt thought. She stared in fascination at the open pit at the bottom of the cliffs and likened it to a lunar landscape. Front end loaders bit into the coarse ash, which would be used to make cleansing agents and cement.

Britt followed the curve of the caldera and spotted the main town of Thera embedded in the rim of the cliffs, its whitewashed buildings incandescent in the late morning sun. Steps zig–zagged up the cliffs from the harbor to the town, with a cable car system spanning the same height. This, too, passed from sight as the plane swooped to the east, then south over dry grape fields and descended to the airstrip on the flat lowlands on the island's eastern side. Britt craned to see the black sand of Kamari Beach, south of the airport, her home for the coming weeks. It remained out of sight.

As the plane dipped down for a landing, Britt looked to the rising land to the west that ended in the drop–offs. What had happened there at the cliff's edge, Britt wondered. Suppose Marcello was wrong. What if someone had killed the photographer by throwing him over the edge? Why would they do it? What had he stumbled on, and would she trip over it, too?

Theodopolis Alevras swung open the wooden gate at the main entrance of the Fira Winery. Just a few miles outside Kamari, the winery squatted in a barren patch of ash, surrounded by fields of grapes and barley. A solitary eucalyptus tree at the side of the building provided scant shade. A guard, slouching in a chair by the door, let his jaws work a freshly lit cigarette as the owner passed.

"You fool," Alevras growled into the receiver of a cordless phone. In his spare hand, a nearly empty beer bottle dangled. "You take care of her on the mainland, you say."

"Yannis screwed up," the voice on the other end said. "Twice."

"Never does he fail for me."

"Listen. I've talked with your father. He agrees. We can't have another death on Santorini. That would seem too suspicious."

"We can have whatever I want," Alevras said. He yanked open the front door and entered the dark interior of the winery's office.

"Do you want Zerakis to send investigators? Or perhaps you'd like to draw in the U.S. government?"

"What do you mean?" Alevras stopped dead. "How did they get involved?"

"Britt Evans had breakfast at the U.S. Embassy. Then, Richard Marcello, an American agent, drove her to the airport. You kill her and I guarantee you'll have so much intelligence crawling in your little kingdom that your head will explode."

"Idiot!" Alevras cried and tossed the phone on the long wooden counter. He tipped back the Spartan bottle and emptied the brew into his mouth. Hung over from the night before, the Greek grimaced at the sour taste.

A cafe owner leaning on the counter, broke off his haggling with the clerk in attendance.

"Your offer is an insult," Alevras declared, muscling the clerk to the side.

"You don't know what it is!" the buyer cried.

"I know you, you cheap rooster. We sell you two cases of wine and you think you deserve bulk rates."

"Where is your head! It's twenty cases a month. You are lucky for that—tourists have one glass and never ask for another. It is rancid vinegar!"

"To wash down your rancid food!"

"What is this? What is this?" Sophia Delopsos jerked open a yellow and burgundy striped curtain at the back office and entered the small square of open space.

"Look at you," Alevras's aunt cried, spitting out the Greek words, "hung–over and unshaven. Move aside."

"You should be out here in the first place," Alevras said, giving way to the thin frame of Mrs. Delopsos. He perched on the clerk's desk and began playing with a sharp spindle as his aunt concluded the deal.

"Your father should see you," Mrs. Delopsos said as soon as the customer walked out the door. She patted her gray hair, swept back severely and clipped in the rear with a silver barrette. "You are a disgrace to your family."

"What are you?" Alevras countered, jabbing the spindle toward the axe–blade face of his mother's sister. "A beggar to the family."

"I take what life gives me, and I am thankful to God for it. But you..."

"But you..." he mocked. He'd spent his childhood listening to his faults. "I have more important business than this..." he eyed the bare walls, the one sign written in Greek, German, and English saying "NO WINE TASTING," and the bars on the dust–covered windows, "...this godforsaken hell–hole." Alevras wagged the little finger of his left hand in his aunt's face. "You are not worth the dirt under my nail!"

Mrs. Delopsos glared at him, then stalked into the back room. The ceiling fan slowly churned the thick air.

"My father, is he still in Athens?" Alevras asked of the graying clerk, an old lackey of his father's.

"Yes, Colonel Alevras is there. He does not know when he will be down. He may go directly to Crete."

The corners of Theo's mouth curved down. "I see. We have a change in plans. I want to delay Friday's shipment."

"Delay it?"

"Yes. The next shipment will be a double one."

"But the risk..."

"The risk is greater if we move our wares now." Alevras retrieved the phone from the counter and dialed the Seaside Pension.

"Hello, my sweetheart," he chirped. "Tell me about the guests the old man has checked in today." He listened intently. "This last one, where is she now?" Alevras grinned. "Take a break. Meet me at the beach and point her out."

The clerk looked blankly at his employer.

"We have a new player on Santorini, an American professor. You see," Alevras said, resting the tip of the spindle on a button of the clerk's shirt, "she is the mouse, and I am the cat. We have a little game to play, and then dinner time."

After checking in at the Seaside, a pension two blocks inland from Kamari Beach, Britt changed into swimwear and headed for the beach. She claimed a coffin–sized rectangle on a patch of sand in front of the Pelican, a taverna of weathered wood. A canopy of vines wrapped around bamboo poles shaded its veranda from the white–hot sun.

Small shops lined the stretch of beach ahead of her, with the expensive Kamari Hotel marking the end of the well–used portion of the beach. Further north, the campgrounds and a narrowing beach curved into low, rocky hills. A plane was lifting above them, taking off from the airport on the other side of the hills.

Heat rose off the beach in searing waves. A hot breeze stirred Britt's black hair off her face and reddened her cheeks. She slipped out of her white terry cloth robe, already damp with perspiration. She smeared sunscreen on her arms and legs, face and neck, and as much of her back as she could reach.

At last, she propped herself on her elbows so she could examine the heights of Mesa Vouno, the mountain rising at the southern end of the beach. Great slabs of rock lay exposed, and tufts of shrubs and burnt grass dotted the simmering surface. It was hell to climb, but Britt knew she'd make at least one trip to the Classical ruins that clung to its top.

The professor surveyed the swell of the waves and the dozen or so sailboards cutting through the sea. One with a sail of bright orange and yellow, rounded the southern prom-ontory formed by the base of Mesa Vouno, which separated Kamari Beach from its sister black beach at Perissa. The rider used a sailful of wind to fly over deep troughs and land on opposite walls of water with a force that would have knocked most surfers into the sea.

The rider, bearing in toward shore, suddenly swung the sail around. The board bit into the water and made a sixty-degree turn. A woman, Britt thought, registering the fullness of the hips encased in a black sleeveless wetsuit marked with a geometric pattern of lime green. The stiff wind blew her blonde hair straight back. Gleaming white goggles masked her face.

Britt put her head down and let the sun beat into her. "Good–bye, Athens," she said under her breath, letting the swirl of the city flow out of her pores. The smell of salt and coconut oil replaced the odor of diesel and sewage. The cries of gulls and the slap of the surf supplanted the roar of traffic. Nearby, a small boy squawked in pain as he hopped from foot to foot across the burning sand. Reaching his parents' blanket, the boy rubbed away his tears, gave Britt a trembling smile, and began to dig a trench.

Time to cool down, Britt thought. At the water's edge, she toed the cold surf, then plunged into deeper water. As she stroked through the sea in a slow crawl, her arms cycling through the water like lazy turbines, her goosebumps smoothed into solid flesh.

Theo Alevras, watching from shore, plotted his strategy.

A quarter mile off shore, Britt dove straight down, twisted around, and pointed herself toward the beach. As she broke the surface, she heard a yelp, then caught a flash of orange as a sail slapped into the water.

The blond windsurfer sputtered to the surface. "Christ," she said, rubbing her nose, "where did you come from? I could've cut you in two."

Britt blew a spout of sea water. "I'm in one piece. How about you?"

The young woman pushed her goggles on top of her head. "My adrenal glands are pretty worked up. Other than that, I'm okay."

"Yeah," Britt said, her heart still thumping, "mine, too." The direct gaze of the stranger startled her. She had large eyes the color of storm clouds, with their depth and density constantly changing. Britt nabbed the yellow board as it drifted toward them, and steered it toward the windsurfer.

"Thanks. You're out quite a ways," she said. "Would you like a lift in?"

"No, thanks," Britt said, letting go of the board. "They work best solo."

"You're a rider?"

"Not like you."

The blonde hoisted herself onto the board. "You can take this baby out sometime. She handles like a coupe."

"Thanks for the offer," Britt said, treading toward the shore.

"No, I mean it. Look, I almost killed you. It's the least I could do. If you see me around, just ask. My name's Cassie." The surfer lowered her goggles, slid her feet into the mid–range straps, hauled up the sail, and was gone.

8

When Britt returned to her blanket, she saw a dark–haired man in a white polo shirt perched on the corner.

"Hello," he said. His black irises swam in red, round eyes.

"Get off my blanket," she said, reaching for her towel.

Theo Alevras squinted into the sun and pulled a captain's hat low over his eyes. "You are a good swimmer, Professor Britt Evans."

Britt, drying off her legs, straightened herself to her full five–and–a–half feet and examined the man sitting with his knees up, leaning back on his hands. She looped the towel around her neck and grabbed an end in each hand. "Who are you?"

"Theo Alevras," he said, sweeping his cap off his head with a muscular arm. "You have been admiring my yacht. Is this not so?" The cap left a circular indentation in his shaggy, black hair.

"No, I haven't." Britt had been so intent on the windsurfer that she hadn't paid much attention to the yacht anchored off shore. Now she shifted her gaze to the lounging craft, its upper cabin of warm, glistening mahogany, the sides an imposing black. A Greek flag fluttered aft.

"The *Praxis*, she's mine. All sixty–two feet of her."

"Congratulations." Britt shifted her inspection from the yacht to the young man seated before her. He appeared to be in his mid–twenties.

"How do you know who I am?" Britt slipped her robe over her strong but tired shoulders, then sat on the opposite corner of the blanket.

He fished for cigarettes in a shirt pocket. His upper arm muscles swelled slightly with the motion, stretching the sleeve bands of his shirt. "Easy. I have a...how do you say this...an 'association' with the Akrotiri excavation. I see the article there about your lectures. Your picture is there. I see your book, too. Forgive me, I didn't read it. Too many words. Too much English."

"Who do you know at the dig?" Britt asked, quickly reassessing the stranger. Her tone had softened appreciably.

He rubbed his hand across the thickening beard on his chin. "Dr. Gavas. Many people. I make special deliveries sometimes to Akrotiri. When do you go there?"

A sail slapped the nearby water. Britt glanced over and saw the windsurfer jump off the sleek board. She hit the sand moments later.

"Theo," the blonde said, "the speed of your pursuit astonishes even me."

"I'm speaking with the professor, please," he said, his shoulders slumping for a second.

"You must be Britt Evans," the windsurfer said. There was no hint of it being a question.

"Yes. I'm beginning to think my name's tatooed on my forehead."

"I thought you looked familiar out there. I'm Cassie Burkhardt." She extended her hand in a firm shake. Her hair was plastered to her head. Small patches of sea foam glimmered at her hairline. "I work at the excavation."

"I've heard your name before—from Bob Collins. I have a letter from him that I'm supposed to give you."

"No hurry." Cassie pointed her strong, tanned face in Theo's direction. "Is he bothering you?"

"Not yet."

"I could tell him to move along." She gave the Greek a pop-eyed look.

Alevras yawned. "I must go." He stood and stretched, all the while looking across the water at his yacht. He nodded to

Britt. "It has been a pleasure. It is always nice to have such a beautiful girl come to this island. I will take you for a good time someday in my yacht before you leave." He grinned at both women, tipped his hat, then sauntered up the beach.

"Good riddance," Cassie said. "I'm sorry Theo was your welcoming committee." The wind had already dried a few strands of fine hair to a rich golden color.

"No need to apologize." The women again inspected each other for a moment. Britt noticed now that Cassie's eyes weren't a solid gray. They had flecks of brown and black. "Please, sit down."

"Can't. I stayed out longer than I should have. I'm taking the afternoon off to run a few errands."

Britt stared at Cassie. "You didn't windsurf from the excavation, did you?"

"Yeah. It's a killer ride. I don't recommend it."

Britt laughed. "I've never heard of anyone who commutes by sailboard!"

"I never thought of it that way." Cassie's face broke into a brilliant, dimpled smile, her white teeth as even as piano keys. "I've only done it a few times—mostly to prove to myself that I can do it. Plus, it's a lot more exciting than driving." She unzipped her wetsuit. "Whew, it's hot. How about dinner tonight?"

"Thanks. I'd like that."

"I'll bring along the other American on the excavation— Jim Larson. He's a hoot."

"Fine," Britt replied, surprised at her disappointment that they would not be dining alone. "I'm at the Seaside..."

"I know," Cassie said. "We'll pick you up at eight."

"Computers. That's what brought us here." Cassie watched as the dark sea extinguished the last orange rays of the sun. The bare light bulbs hanging from the veranda of the restaurant in Thera took on a sudden intensity. "That's a pretty sterile reason for coming to Greece, I suppose."

"I prefer to think of us as refugees from Silicon Valley," Jim Larson said, setting his wine glass carefully between the bread basket and his plate. In the dim light, his red hair almost matched the color of the wine. "We were once peons in the vast empire of DeLouise-Benson, Inc. Now we're Santorin royalty performing magical tricks on a monitor. The natives lay fruit at our feet. Crowds divide as we pass."

Britt and Cassie exchanged a glance.

"All right, so we're still on the DB payroll," Jim added with a scowl.

"And DB gets a tax deduction for its contribution to world culture." Cassie raised her wine glass in a toast to the invisible corporate empire.

"But we, my dear Cassie, get the fresh air of Greece and the privilege of contributing to the archaeological canon. Surely, Professor Evans, you appreciate us."

"I do, indeed."

"Before we came here," Cassie said, "Jim was your basic hotshot programmer and I was a hacker."

"Nerd. She was a nerd," Jim whispered loudly to Britt. "She had glasses so thick Mount Palomar was after her."

Britt and Cassie laughed. Jim feigned seriousness and stared haughtily into the dark caldera.

"Were you two involved in DB's Arizona project?"

"Just me," Cassie said, impressed at Britt's knowledge. "I worked on the prototype computer system—we set up the programs for data collection, data integration and analysis, the cataloguing of artifacts—stuff like that."

"'Stuff like that.' She was brilliant, Professor. The star of DB for an entire quarter. Why they even wrote about her in the in-house monthly and gave her a dinner for two."

"At the company cafeteria," Cassie laughed.

Britt cocked her head like an inquisitive bird. Unfamiliar with the corporate world, she couldn't tell if they were joking. "So you both pulled up roots for what—a couple of years—to come here for this excavation?"

"Eighteen months. I think the natives will be ready to take over the project by the end of summer. They're wily creatures. They learn fast." Jim picked up the empty wine bottle and caught the waiter's eye. "See what I mean?" he said, when the waiter nodded and spun on his heels to fetch a new bottle.

"Dr. Gavas mentioned that you're writing a few articles on the Minoan culture," Cassie said.

"The Minoans and Minoan–influenced cultures. I'm exploring some concepts about the interpretation of the natural world by prehistoric cultures."

"Companion pieces to your book?"

"In a way. Mainly I'm following up on some ideas that I had while writing it."

"Well, the data base is all set up. Right now Jim and I are working on stratigraphy. At any given area of the site we can peel away the layers. Every fact about each layer is fully described and recorded. The artifacts themselves are sent to the museum here in Thera."

By the time they neared the end of the second bottle of wine, Cassie had zipped up her fuchsia windbreaker and Britt had pulled on a navy sweater. Jim alone remained untouched by the chilly evening air and continued to sit in his short–sleeved tattersall shirt. He had also imbibed the largest share of the alcohol.

"Friends," he cried, clutching the now empty bottle, "it's time for departure. We have work to do—pots to dig, data to enter, manuscripts to write!" He closed his eyes and swayed.

"Jim, my boy" Cassie said, as she rose from her chair and eased him out of his, "you're not going to be fit for any civilization tomorrow—Minoan or modern."

"You two go on ahead," Britt said, "I'll get the bill."

She caught up with Cassie and Jim on a twisted, whitewashed street. Most shops had closed for the night. A few merchants were sweeping dirt from their doorsteps.

As they passed a gift store, Jim yanked the women to a halt. He squinted at a display window where a cloth of red velvet concealed valuable items.

"No, you don't," Cassie said.

But Jim lurched through the open door, flinging off Cassie and Britt. He swayed like a willow in the middle of the shop. Distorted reflections of him played on the glass doors of cases lining the walls, their shelves holding delicately painted replicas of Minoan and Classic pottery. Jim focused on a woman thumbing through a pile of receipts and punching numbers into a calculator.

"Irene, my love!" Jim cried, arms outstretched.

The dark mop of hair snapped up. "Papa!" the young woman called, her eyes like large drops of unsweetened chocolate.

A plump man with graying hair stepped through an open door at the rear of the shop. Irene froze, her thick fingers stuck in their work.

"Good evening, Mr. Kazantas," Jim said, using his arms to balance himself.

"You go home, now," the mustachioed proprietor said. "Come back tomorrow."

"What? You're refusing me?" Jim tipped backward, then steadied himself. "I have never refused you."

Kazantas grinned wildly at Cassie and Britt. "You take your friend home? Come back when he is not so..." The merchant held out his hands and made them tremble.

"Come back, come back," Jim snorted. "Why bother? I can never see her without a chhhhhaperon."

"You need a chaperon," Cassie said, grabbing him by the arm. "Come on, Britt, let's get him out of here."

Britt latched on to his other arm. He seemed pliant now, the moment of confrontation sapping his strength.

"A touching display, Jim," Cassie said as the women steered him down the street. "I'm sure your future father–in–law was mightily impressed."

"He needs me," Jim mumbled. "He needs me."

"If I were Jim, I'd probably go on a few benders myself," Cassie said after the women had dropped him off at the dormitory at the Akrotiri site. "He's never been lucky with women, then he gets here and every family on this island sees him as their ticket to America. The cruel twist is that he can't have sex with their daughters outside of marriage."

"So he's engaged now?"

"Yep. He has the in–laws now, but still no sex. Poor guy," Cassie said, laughing softly. "He's a whiz in the programming department, but outside of his computer, every choice leads him down a wrong path."

Britt shifted in her seat. "Tell me, why are you staying in Kamari instead of at the dorm?"

"I never got around to seriously settling in there. It was shut down during the off–season when I first came here, so I stayed in Thera. Which was where I needed to be anyway, since I spent most of my time in the museum. Then, last summer, when the dorm opened, I stayed for a week. That was enough. The boys were as bad as the bugs, no creature comforts, and most importantly, no beach. Akrotiri is my work, but I'm not willing to sacrifice everything for it."

"So you moved to Kamari?"

"Yep. Paulos Bountourakis and his wife, Maria, own—owned—a pension in Kamari so the arrangements were easy, and the rent cheap enough so my DB managers didn't squawk."

The reference to Bountourakis palled the conversation. The brown Golf skimmed over the narrow road. The landscape, barely visible in the waning moon, appeared jagged and bleak.

"That's where his body was found." Cassie pointed a long white finger at the void to the left of the road. "Down below there." The car sped past the site.

Britt craned around, then facing Cassie, leaned against the door. Her hair, hanging out the open window, whipped itself into a hundred tangles. "Did you know him well?"

Cassie nodded.

"You were good friends?"

"I wouldn't say good. We were sort of pals. Not really close, though. I saw him a lot, living at the pension. He taught me a good deal about photography. He has—had—his own darkroom at his place. It's been locked up most of the time since he died. Maria says no one wants to touch the possessions of a dead man. Poor woman." A pale ray of moonlight turned a few strands of her hair to a subdued gold.

The Golf veered north, heading for the connecting roads to the eastern side of the island.

"So what besides computers brought you to Santorini?" Britt asked.

"Truth be told, adventure. A Greek island sounded exciting and romantic. A paradise. It was, for about five days. Then I wondered what the hell I'd gotten myself into." Cassie gripped the steering wheel at the twelve o'clock position. "Don't get me wrong. I love Greece and all that, but who wants to live on an ash pile? Anyway, what I had done, I realized after some time, was escape a messy relationship."

"Ah–hah," Britt said.

"Not very noble, I admit." The car changed course again, streaking past a small, darkened village. Its whitewashed buildings glowed in the moonlight like fluorescent boxes. "He wanted marriage. I didn't. There are just so many ways a person can say no. I think he finally got the message when I left the country."

"Sounds like he had it bad," Britt said, feeling a twinge of empathy for the spurned suitor. She could understand why he had been smitten. Cassie was certainly a compelling woman.

"I know. The poor guy showed up at the departure gate at the airport to see me off."

"I hope he's not still pining."

"No, thank heaven. My mom sent an engagement announcement she had clipped out of the paper. He's getting married in September."

"Speaking of letters," Britt said, reaching into her fanny pack and extracting an envelope. "Here. Bob Collins sent this by special delivery."

"Oh, jeez," Cassie said, taking the letter and flinging it on the dashboard, "more trouble."

9

"As before, you have my trust," Dr. Alfonsos Gavas said, concluding his initial meeting with Britt in which he had set the boundaries for her research. Gavas, in charge of the Akrotiri excavation for several years, was a popular man. His main concern was the excavation itself and its family of diggers, rather than an academic empire.

"Come," he said, rising from a dilapidated chair in a shanty–town cube of an office. Stacks of dusty books and photographs towered toward the roof. White handkerchiefs smudged with dried sweat dotted the clutter. "I show you how our work has progressed since your last visit. Then I leave you on your own."

They strolled through the dusty streets, deserted except for occasional strings of tourists lead by a guide. Off to the side in roped–off areas, workers knelt over artifacts protruding from the camel–colored soil.

"So, what's new since I saw you last?" the American asked.

"These last years have been busy. Much cataloging—it's all computer now. Your Americans help with that." The director patted his stomach, which had expanded a few inches with middle–age. "Some of us work in the new museum in Thera. Organizing and cataloging. We help also with the old artifacts—the Minoan Exhibition. It was transferred here a few years ago from the National Museum in Athens."

They shuffled along like tourists through the winding streets. When they reached the room containing the grave of Dr. Marinatos, both scholars stopped. Their feet pointed at the mound of earth that held the man who had spearheaded the excavation back in the days when the site was just another field of grapevines at the southern bend of Santorini. An accident at the dig had taken his life in 1967.

"You have heard about our recent loss, I'm sure."

"Bountourakis. Yes. What exactly happened?" Britt turned from the grave, which was blanketed with daisies, poppies, daffodils, and sprigs of evergreen. Her gaze rested for one intense moment on Gavas, then lifted as he stood silently in thought. Above them, acres of tin stretched into a crude, functional ceiling designed to protect the ruins from the elements. Panels of opaque plastic let in light; a sturdy steel network of beams supported the entire structure.

With his thick fingers, Gavas removed his black–framed glasses and rubbed his eyes. "Only Paulos could say. We know only that he fell from the cliffs between here and Thera. We think maybe he shoot the caldera in moonlight. Maybe the windmill against the moon—that would make a pretty picture, eh? But who knows?"

They ambled on, taking small, slow steps, and entered the roped–off administration section with its rows of file cabinets and desks. Britt spied Cassie at a computer in a far corner, typing like a madwoman. She allowed herself to think briefly of the previous night, and of how much she enjoyed Cassie's company. No doubt about it, her stay on Santorini was going to be fun.

"Ah," Gavas said, as he passed a row of four–drawer vertical files. He picked up a heavy folder resting on top of the end file. "Here, Britt, the first batch of extracts."

"Good. These should keep me busy for a lifetime or two." Britt excused herself to the director, then settled at a corner worktable to examine the documents of the excavation.

Dr. Gavas, Britt thought, was his usual affable self. How absurd to think he'd have anything to do with the theft of artifacts. The only one sleazy enough to do it, she thought, was Theo Alevras. She'd keep an eye on him. She'd... Britt paused. Damn you, Rich Marcello, she thought. I'm doing exactly what you wanted me to do. You knew all along that I would!

To spite the embassy official, Britt opened the thick folder and willed herself to forget Athens, the strange man in the street, the dilapidated truck that almost ran down Nicki and her, and the embassy official who had so superbly maneuvered himself into her life.

At lunchtime in Thera the following Monday, Britt sat alone at an outdoor cafe. She licked an oversized blue stamp and flattened it on a postcard of a monastery brilliantly white against a cobalt sky. She knew her aunt would appreciate a note from her, accompanied by a touch of religion. Holding up the card, Britt compared the real sky to the picture; the true stretch of heaven matched the fake, deep and cloudless. A small ferry carrying a freight of sightseers bobbed from the port far below to the cluster of black islands in the distance.

A couple of flies jigged around crumbs from a delicately crusted spinach pie called spanakopita. Britt slid the plate to the side and a waiter cleared it. Only a sweating bottle of lemonade stayed on the gingham tablecloth, and a wine bottle with its neck plugged by a well-dripped candle.

Britt set her pen to the backside of another postcard. *Dear Mom.* What should I tell her? Britt considered, laying the felt tip next to the card. Don't worry. I'm not lonely here. I'm finding friends. A friend, actually. Yes, she's a woman. I like her a lot. She windsurfs to work and has shaggy blond hair. It sweeps back off her face in a sort of unkempt, yet classy way. She has a few nicely defined muscles, and a slow, but purposeful gait. Maybe it comes from island living. She's intelligent and knows all about computers. Yes, I'm going on a bit, aren't I? No, I'm not falling in love. I wouldn't do anything so foolish. She's straight and I'll bet she has men standing in line for her. She's strictly off–limits on that count alone. Then there's the fact that she's here for the rest of the summer, then she'll be going back to California. And she seems pretty techy for me. I love art; I can't see spending my life with someone talking about bytes or bits or whatever they are. So, there's nothing to worry about. I'm being careful as usual. I've learned to be. Britt picked up the pen. *Having a great time. Getting lots of work done.*

As Britt set a period at the end of a tired sentence, someone brushed against the table. The metal legs scratched across the stone walk, and Britt's felt pen streaked across her postcard.

"Mr. Kazantas!" she cried, recognizing the rotund shopkeeper from her first night on the island. His daughter followed close behind.

Kazantas's dark eyes, surrounded by folds of olive skin, ran over her blankly.

"We met last week in your shop," Britt said.

Irene, who had recognized the American instantly, spoke sharply to her father.

"So my daughter says. My memory," the merchant said, pressing a finger to his temple, "sometimes she is forgetful like an old stubborn mule. You are the new American at Akrotiri."

"That's right," Britt said, holding out her hand and introducing herself. The father's grip snapped like a jaw; the daughter's was not offered.

"I'm sorry we had to meet under those circumstances," she continued, flashing her most winsome smile.

"Yes, yes," Mr. Kazantas said, returning the expression. "Such things happen. A boy so far from home. Sometimes very homesick. It is not so good."

"I'm glad he's made friends such as you," Britt said.

"We are lucky for him," Irene replied. Her father smiled benignly at his daughter, but his eyes were frigid black circles. "When we are married and I go to America, I can set up a shop like my father's. We will be very happy."

"That's quite an enterprise for you and Jim," Britt said.

"Oh, my bothers would help. They..."

"Come, come," Mr. Kazantas replied, "we keep the lady from her letters, from friends anxious to hear from her."

"But papa..."

"A pleasure," the shopkeeper said, as he steered Irene from the table, his fingers digging into his daughter's arm.

The soft wood of a number two pencil yielded again to Britt's canines and took on another row of indentations. Yes! Britt said to herself, tapping the pockmarked implement on a pile of note cards. The first milestone of her self-imposed schedule was a breath away. The last few days of hard work had paid off: nearing the end of phase one of her research, she needed to track down just a few loose ends in the basement of the Thera Museum. One end refused to be found.

Printouts scattered on the long worktable listed every artifact connected to animals uncovered and catalogued from the Akrotiri excavation. Lines and circles, jottings trailed by exclamation points or question marks, and references to other listings decorated the pages. Two dozen eight-by-five index cards lay nearby, the result of her long morning of research.

Plucking up a note card, Britt swung around on her stool and rested her elbows on the table as she surveyed the cabinets. She reread her notes: "Monkey motif: ewer: Cycladic; polychrome; breasted." According to the catalog, the water pitcher should be in the cabinet directly across from her. But she hadn't found it there, nor in any of the other cabinets along the white plaster wall. Britt had checked each carefully.

This could be it, she thought, thinking of Rich Marcello's suggestion that Bountourakis had stumbled onto a smuggling ring. She felt warm drops of sweat roll down to her waist. It may be nothing, she reasoned. The ewer could be missing for a number of reasons. Don't jump to conclusions, she said trying to calm herself; remember scholarly detachment and objectivity. After all, it's possible for someone to make a mistake or be careless. It seemed plausible. But not probable, given the high level of professionalism she had seen at the excavation and here in the museum.

"You look puzzled."

Britt started. "Hi, Jim."

"Having trouble finding something?"

The professor drummed her fingers against her note cards as she thought. "As a matter fact, I am," she confessed. "There's a monkey ewer that seems to be hiding from me."

"The little bugger. Do you have its catalog number?"

"Here." Britt handed him the note card.

Jim ran his long fingers along the edges of the card. "I think I know that one. You've looked everywhere?"

"Every place I could think of."

Jim patted the card against his lips. "Some dolt probably took it to another room and forgot to note it. This place is clinical proof that Alzheimer's is contagious. Staff members can't button their shirts without help."

"Are you saying that the museum is in disarray?"

"Well, no. Just that people are careless."

"What's going on?"

"If you ask me, they're too busy thinking about making money. Half the workers here have at least two businesses on the side, grubbing after tourist dollars so they can make a pile and move off this godforsaken lava rock. They've got their wives running pensions or cleaning them, and their kids in the fields or waiting tables or both."

"Aren't you striking a bit close to home there?"

Jim's freckled face compressed with confusion.

"I hear you and Irene plan to open a branch of Mr. Kazantas's store in the U.S."

"Where did you hear that?"

"Irene. She and her father bumped into me at lunch yesterday. Literally. Was it a secret?"

"No. It's an idiotic fantasy. Created by an idiot to serve idiots."

"Not enamored of the in–laws, eh?"

"The old man is an authority on the world, and he's never been off this stinking island. He has no idea of commerce in the Bay area. Of course, he's got Irene starry–eyed about the scheme."

"Do I still hear wedding bells?"

"Sometimes they sound pretty tinny." Jim fingered the note card on the table. "How soon do you need to see this ewer?"

"Soon." Noticing Jim's eyes widen, she retreated. "I can wait a bit, though."

"I'll check it out. It's bound to turn up. Listen, I need to finish debugging the program I'm working on right now. I'll track this down later. Don't worry about it."

"I won't," Britt said. It wasn't really a lie, she told herself. She wouldn't worry about that one piece of pottery. But she sure as hell would worry about what its disappearance could mean and if she would keep that information within the archaeology family or tell authorities in Athens.

10

On her knees at the southern end of the Akrotiri site, Britt carefully scraped back the soil from an emerging wall. Dust hung heavily in the hot, still air. It seeped into Britt's khaki shorts and clung to her hair and skin. She started in surprise at a sudden, warm pressure on her shoulder.

"Sorry. I didn't mean to scare you." Cassie squatted next to her.

Britt rolled back and collapsed in the dirt. She wiped her sweaty forehead with a row of smudged knuckles and laughed. "That's okay. I needed a good jolt—I was beginning to feel hypnotized. If only I could concentrate this hard on the dust in my house."

"You and me both." Cassie's dimples dug into her cheeks. "Couldn't stay away from the trowels, huh?"

"No. I thought I'd contribute some labor to pay for the lunches I've been eating here."

"That's thoughtful."

"Not for my back. What's up?"

"Athinios port called. A printer we've been waiting for has just been unloaded. It's sitting on the dock. I could send one of the guys to pick it up, but I'd like to get away. Interested in coming along?"

"Love to."

They sped along the Akrotiri road lined with fields of grape vines. Hazy wisps of moisture churned over the cold waters of the caldera, shaded by its own cliffs. Drawn by the warm air overhead, clouds of water vapor twisted upwards from the sea. A fine mist moved inland and crept down the eastern slope onto the planes below Thera. From this distance, the town's distinct, white buildings seemed wrapped in a heavy, somber sleep.

The breeze from the car's movement provided faint relief from the pressing humidity. Even the notes from a Janet Jackson tape seemed to clog in the speakers.

"You know," Cassie said, sweeping the hair off her forehead, "despite my complaints, I'm going to miss this island. There's no where else like it on earth."

"That's true," Britt smiled.

"It's starting to hit me that I'll be leaving in a couple of months."

"I'd think you'd be anxious to get back to California."

"Actually, I'm not sure where I'll be." Cassie glanced at Britt, then locked her eyes back on the road as a green and yellow tour bus approached them on the narrow lane. "My old department at DB was eliminated about six months ago—part of a ten percent downsizing of the company. I'm on a nationwide placement list for internal DB job openings. I could wind up cranking code in Chicago or doing graphics in Buffalo...if I even stay with the company."

"That doesn't sound very secure."

Cassie let out a playful cackle. "I prefer to think of it as having a flexible future."

A few miles up the road, they veered left and began a descent along the switchbacks leading down to the harbor of Athinios.

The dock, dirty and smelly, had two ships moored. One was a blue and white commercial ferry from Athens, disgorged already of tourists. The other, almost of equal size and with peeling red paint, had its wooden gangplank down. Dozens of small trucks lined the cargo bay, but only a handful near the opening had drivers. A few of them tried to coax their engines to life.

The crate with the printer had been unloaded and stood now to one side of the docking area. Cassie went into the small administrative office to sign for the delivery. Britt waited outside, leaning against the car and watching the nearby activity at the cargo ship. Gulls circled overhead, examining the scene for edible scraps. One landed on a post that held the freighter's rope, squawked some complaints, then dropped a white glob on the dock.

A refrigerated trailer truck rolled slowly down the plank from the freighter, maneuvering with care over the raised horizontal boards. On the door of the truck were the words "Crescent Vineyard" in bold, Greek letters with a crescent and a bunch of red grapes painted beneath .

A Mercedes screeched to a halt next to Cassie's Volkswagen. A lanky man with a two–day growth of beard and a week's accumulation of dirt, jumped out and yelled to the dock hands standing at the mouth of the ship's opening. He looked at Britt, then at the brown Golf.

"Cassie's car? She is here?"

"Inside." Britt pointed to the dock office.

"Ah. You friends? I am Artemios."

Britt introduced herself. "Is this your shipment?"

Another truck began descending the plank. The Greek yelled at the driver, who raised his hand in greeting.

"Yes. It is for the winery."

"The Fira Winery?"

"Ah, you know it. Do you know Theo?"

"We've met." Britt pointed at the trucks. "More supplies for the winery?"

"Grapes."

"Grapes? Don't they grow them here?"

"Some. Not enough. We must ship some in."

"So they come from the Crescent Vineyard. Where's that?"

Artemios adjusted his navy fisherman's cap. "You ask many questions. It is on Crete. Outside Heraklion."

"A problem here?" Theo Alevras asked. He stepped between Britt and her instant friend.

Britt hadn't seen the Captain since their encounter on the beach ten days previously. His bloodshot eyes had cleared up, but the sneer on his face persisted. He reeked of a spicy aftershave.

"So, professor, again we meet. I do not see you for a long time."

"I've been busy."

"Busy! You are in the land of the sun! You must enjoy yourself!"

"Don't worry about it, Theo."

The yacht owner bared his teeth. "But I must. You are a guest on Santorini. Does my worker bother you? I pay him to work not chatter." He turned to the dock hand and regaled him with a rush of Greek.

"My god, Britt," Cassie said, sliding up to the professor, "I leave you alone for three minutes and look what happens. Come on. Let's load our printer. Grab that end, will you?"

"Come! Come! Come!" Artemios shouted at them, breaking off the argument. He and Alevras scrambled to help them.

Cassie winked at Britt as they hoisted the box into the hatchback without a grunt. "Thanks anyway, guys," she said. "I think we're all set." Cassie rifled through a thick packet of papers. She paused. "Hold on. I'm missing a receipt. I'll be back."

Britt slammed the hatch door down, then decided to stroll the length of the small dock. Before she had taken five steps, Artemios joined her.

They stopped in front of the ship that had brought the grapes from Crete. A few cars bumped down the steep plank. High above, a crane was unloading crates of produce. A piercing whistle came from a stevedore standing at the top of the plank to guide the payload. He chatted nonchalantly with Theo, who stood next to him.

"You watch for the operator," Artemios said, pointing to the crane. "He is young—very new. He comes from the shops in Thera, but thinks he knows everything. Sometimes he swings wild."

"Thanks." Britt took in the operator, perched in a tiny, open–air cab, working a series of levers. He wore a headband of striped cloth. Deep, familiar eyes glared out from a round, babyish face.

"All done!" Cassie shouted, waving a sheet of paper as she headed for the car. Britt turned, and at that moment, the crane jerked dangerously. Its payload, a crate the size of a refrigerator, swung out in a wide arch over the side of the ferry. The boom snapped sideways, and the cargo accelerated directly toward Britt.

"Look out!" Cassie cried, knocking her companion to the side. Britt went down on one knee just as the wooden container swooshed by her head, its breeze stirring her hair.

"Are you okay?" Cassie asked. She bent down and put an arm around Britt's shoulder to help her up. The operator snapped the boom up, and with a terrible grinding of gears, the crate rose skyward and swung overhead like a pendulum.

"Fine," Britt said, bending over to dust herself and hide her blush of embarrassment. "Thanks."

Cassie turned from Britt toward the ferry. "What the hell do you thing you're doing?" she shouted at the operator.

Alevras thudded down the plank, his eyes bulging in rage. Spotting the young man behind the controls, he furiously shook his fists. The crane operator jumped from the machine in panic, leaving the crate continuing its precarious swing. Theo disappeared into the maw of the vessel, giving chase.

"Come on," Cassie said, wheeling Britt around by her shoulders, "let's leave. I don't want to see what Theo does to the kid."

"Me either." As they drove through the open gates of the harbor, Britt dusted dirt from her legs under Cassie's watchful eye.

"Sorry to push you like that," Cassie said. "Sure you're okay?"

"Fine. I just need to wipe a little cut," Britt said as she tugged a tissue from her fanny pack. She dabbed at the blood seeping from a scrape on her knee, all the while thinking how much she had liked Cassie's arm around her. That sensation had almost been worth the injury. "Artemios said that those trucks had grapes for the Fira Winery. I didn't realize it was such a big operation."

"It's not, according to Napa Valley standards. Still, it's the biggest one on the island. I'm surprised Theo hasn't pointed that out to you yet."

"He hasn't gotten beyond the glory of his yacht. Artemios gave me the scoop on it."

Cassie made a face, then snapped in a new tape. Eurotech disco thumped through the speakers. "Theo once told me that they use grapes from several of the islands. It's the special blend that gives their wine its distinctive taste."

"Interesting," Britt said thoughtfully. "That poor kid who was operating the crane will be hurting for a week if Theo catches up with him."

"I didn't realize that any of the Kazantas boys were working the docks." Cassie slowed the car as she met a bus bulging with departing tourists. The top of the bus was loaded with backpacks and luggage.

"Kazantas? He was Irene's brother?"

"Right. Soon to be Jim's brother–in–law." She gunned the engine. "Love these Santorini roads!" she shouted, roaring to the top of the cliffs.

11

The next day, Jim Larson swung a maroon Toyota into a dog leg turn and jammed it into the north stall of the dormitory garage. Britt, wheeling her Vespa from its perch in the building's shade, waited for the rolling clouds of dust to dissipate.

"Hey, are you going to the museum?" Jim yelled, as he jumped from the car and slammed the door. AKROTIRI EXCAVATION was stencilled in an eye-popping white on the driver's door.

"Wasn't planning to," Britt said, as she mounted her scooter. "Should I?"

Jim hesitated. "It's up to you. I was just there. That ewer turned up this morning—the monkey one you couldn't find the other day."

"Great! Where was it?"

"On a shelf in the back work room. Some grad student probably left it there."

"Who found it?"

"God himself—Dr. Gavas—conjured it up. Luck of the Greeks."

"Did he know it was missing?"

"Don't think so. Anyway, it's back in the cabinet where it should be."

"I'll look for it first thing Monday. Thanks, Jim." Britt stomped the start pedal.

The engine coughed and held on the second kick. Well, Britt thought to herself as she purred up the gravel one-laner to the main road, no stolen artifacts. This time.

Once past the village of Akrotiri, a quaint settlement of white and pale blue houses imbedded in a steep hillside, she nudged the scooter into third gear. The wind in her face and hair gave her an exhilarating sense of freedom. She had no plans for the evening...and nothing but a long, hot, lazy weekend ahead.

To her left lay the great volcanic crater; to the right a spread of grape vines, the bunches of green leaves evenly spaced in the smoldering gray fields. Low walls made of iron–red, black, and gray volcanic rock separated rows of vines from the small squares of barley fields, the grain already threshed.

Britt impulsively pulled off the road. When the Vespa finally rattled to a stop, the professor was left with the eerie silence that often accompanies magnificent natural spectacles. Perched on the rim of the giant cliffs streaked with mineral deposits, she could see far to the west, where the navy sea reflected the descending sun in a spangle of flashing lights. She peeked over the edge of the gray, dusty cliffs to the ash mines. It was a long way down, like looking from the top of a skyscraper to the street below. To the north, men in hardhats set about storing their equipment for the weekend.

Funny, she thought, settling back from the cliff's edge, how a spectacle like this made her feel such a small part of nature, and that death would be like a tear absorbed into the ocean. The reality, though, would be quite a different thing, she considered. What had Paulos Bountourakis thought as he tumbled down the face of the cliff? He probably hadn't marvelled at the Great Cosmos that he was about to smash into.

Bounty. Britt hadn't thought about him in a couple of days, she realized with a touch of guilt. Had she discovered anything that suggested his death was other than an accident? No. Had she even seen anything suspicious? Not really. The missing ewer? It hadn't been missing after all. If Rich Marcello were to call her—for she certainly would not call him—she'd have nothing of substance to report. Would he be interested in hearing that Theo Alevras, who fancied himself a playboy, seemed a shady but harmless soul wandering the seas in his yacht? And the Kazantas family? Rich would no doubt tell her that the ambition of in–laws was not criminal, though god knows it should be.

A car skidded to a stop behind her. As Britt turned, Cassie poked her head out the window of her Golf. Behind her stood the ghostly carcass of an abandoned windmill, eroding in the element it had been built to harness. "Transport problems?" she asked, pointing to the low–slung Vespa.

"No," Britt shouted into the wind. "I'm here for the view." The professor patted the ground next to her. "Come on, join me."

Cassie snapped off the engine. "You know, I haven't stopped along here since Bounty died," she said, lowering herself to the hard embankment. "It's time that I did. Want some?" She held out a sweating Coke for Britt.

"Thanks." Britt took a swallow and rolled the cold can across her forehead. "Feels good. Inside and out."

A mule's plaintive cry rose from somewhere below them. It started as a baby's wail, then broke into breathy sobs. The women fell silent, each hanging her gaze on the horizon, far beyond the brooding black islands.

"Have any plans for the weekend?" Britt asked.

"Nope. Now that Bob's out of my life—I hope—my weekends are mine. Not that he was such a bother, really. He let me have my space—I could be out on the waves all afternoon, and he'd find ways to amuse himself."

"What happened with you two anyway?"

"Oh, I don't know. I'd been having second thoughts about the relationship for several months. I guess I got bored. I was never in love with him anyway. Nor he with me."

"Really? From the look on his face when he handed me that letter in Athens, I'd say he was rather smitten."

Britt felt Cassie's eyes burn into her.

"That surprises me," Cassie said. "I never would have thought so. I heard he's been elbowing a couple of new girlfriends at the School. Maybe he was feeling guilt or remorse."

"About what? You broke it off."

"He was a real shit about Bounty, then the poor guy dies." Cassie picked up a stone and rubbed it between her fingers like a worry bead. "I think Bob was jealous of him. He thought Bounty and I were making it."

Britt's eyebrows shot to the top of her forehead.

"We weren't, of course. In fact, it never came up between us. If I had to put money on it, I think he was gay—he was kind of femmy. His wife, Maria, was probably just an ignorant cover. Maybe not. They did seem to have genuine affection for each other."

"It wouldn't be the first marriage of facade."

"I'm sure." She tipped the can back and poured some soda down her throat. "Bob was jealous, though he had no cause to be. I keep pretty much to myself around here. The tourists are into each other, not the fifty–hours–a–week grinders like me."

"Tell me more about what happened with Bountourakis."

Cassie ran a thumbnail along a white swirl on the can. "I have a bad feeling that there's more to his death than we know. Bob has given me a hard time about that. You know, 'women's intuition.'" She shifted her focus to the seam between the sky and sea. "I think Bob was glad that he died."

The programmer caught Britt's penetrating look. "He didn't have anything to do with it, if that's what you're thinking. He was here that weekend, but he went back to

Athens late Sunday afternoon, long before Bounty had dinner, much less left the pension to take pictures."

"Uh–huh."

"You see," Cassie said, setting the soda to the side, "Bounty wasn't even supposed to be here. He told me after dinner that night that he was going down to the beach— Kamari Beach—to shoot some pictures. In fact, I saw him get in his car and drive down the beach road. He never planned to come to this side of the island. But the next day, the miners found his body down there." Cassie pointed a lean finger toward the edge of the cliff.

"Why would Bounty drive? The beach is only two blocks from his place, and parking there is impossible."

Cassie blinked hard. "I never thought of that. Maybe he didn't want to carry his equipment."

"Maybe," Britt replied, unconvinced. She reached for the Coke and took another sip. "Did you mention your concerns to the police?"

"Sure. They shrugged and said, 'He changed his mind.' So, I've done my civic duty," she said bitterly.

"Like your namesake."

"Let's hope not. Actually, I was named for my grandmother Cassandra." Cassie finished the Coke and crushed the can. "How about you, Brittany?"

"That was my mother's doing," she confessed, slipping her eyes away to escape Cassie's bright, quick appraisal.

"She didn't breed spaniels, did she?"

Britt laughed. "No. I was named for Brittany, France. My mom's people are from there."

A car whizzed by, whipping up clouds of dust. "Your parents must be proud of you," Cassie said, waving her arms to clear the air.

"Yes and no. They're proud of my career, but they despair of my being an old maid, which by their definition means being without a man."

"Old maid!" Cassie hooted. "God, I thought that term died decades ago. Listen, this will be the one and only prediction I'll ever make—you won't wind up alone. How's that?"

"I don't believe you," Britt laughed. "What about your family?"

"Born and raised in Palo Alto. The folks are still there. Dad works at a small computer firm—he's a hardware guy— and my mom's a part-time writing instructor at Stanford."

"Miss them?"

"Some. We keep in touch. I miss the wave action more. The surf here is child's play, but at least there's a great wind for sailboarding."

"A beach bum, huh?"

"I spent the school summers on the beach chasing the waves and the boys."

"I bet you caught them."

"Plenty of both." Cassie's dimples flashed. "I guess I've been pretty cavalier about it all. You screw one up, there's always another rolling in behind.

A tourist bus rumbled by, sending another barrage of dust billowing over the women.

"Jeez," Cassie said, "let's get out of here."

"Where?"

"There's a great place down the road for dinner. Then the beach for a beer. Maybe the Disco Volcano after."

While the sun made a dazzling descent in the west, edging past the burnt islands in the darkening caldera, at Kamari the light drained simply and without spectacle from the eastern seaboard, pulling in its wake an ever–darkening canopy.

Wearing jeans and cotton blouses, Britt and Cassie strad-dled high wooden stools. The open–air bar centered a row of tavernas lining the street parallel to the beach. Lights beamed everywhere, strung along roofs and through evergreen trees. Tourists, relaxed and satiated after a day in the sun, hunched over tables and lounged in chairs. Outside a large starfish hung from a rafter, swinging in the breeze like a horse thief.

The women gazed at the sea. Small whitecaps sprinted to shore, slapping the beach with a muted splash. For a brief moment, the entire Mediterranean pulled back for a quick breath, then blew curls of water toward shore. Britt felt absolutely and utterly content, sitting there with Cassie.

"Hey," Cassie said, "a yacht."

Britt ran her eyes along the northeast horizon. In the distance, a craft wedged itself through the black waters, its portholes ablaze. It leaned in toward the land, making a sharp turn toward Kamari Beach. The sleek lines looked familiar.

"It's the *Praxis.*"

Cassie squinted. "So it is. Theo's probably on his way to make a sperm deposit."

The stars winked above; the wind fell to a soft breeze, then intensified. Several men ran to and fro on the deck of the yacht. A couple of sailors tore the tarp off a motor boat that was secured to the starboard.

"Isn't it an unusual time for a visit?" Britt asked.

"Not for Theo. The man has no sense of time—or of how the world operates. It never occurs to him that most people have to go to work in the morning. He believes in partying around the clock." Cassie checked her watch. "Speaking of partying, time to hit the disco."

The throbbing beat of dance music sounded at the entrance of the Disco Volcano, a small stucco bar on the north end of town and in a block from the beach. Britt slipped her Vespa into a row of scooters and mopeds at the side of the building, while Cassie dug in her pockets for the cover charge of a hundred and fifty drachmas.

Inside, couples gyrated on the parquet dance floor under flashing lights and swirling smoke. Britt surveyed the room, searching for a table. The alcoves, stuffed with revelers, rocked with raucous laughter; college–aged tourists mingled at the long wooden bar or propped themselves against the mirrored walls.

"I think we're too late to find a table," Cassie shouted. "Maybe not," she added, spotting arms flagging them. "Jim's over there. With Irene and one of her brothers. Looks like Artemios is there too—you remember—from the dock? What do you say?"

"I'm game," said Britt.

The group slid their chairs around a table about the size of a bird bath. Artemios stole two chairs from a nearby table, temporarily abandoned for the dance floor.

"This is my brother, Georgios," Irene said.

"Hi," Britt said, extending her hand to the young man. Dark marks streaked down the left side of his face, and a swollen eye blinked pathetically at the American. "I remember you from Athinios. You almost cracked my head open."

"It was an accident. Many apologies for it. I am happy you are not hurt."

"Looks like Theo caught up with you," Cassie said, shimmying her chair closer to the table.

Georgios placed a thick hand on his inflated face. "Yes. He gives me his fist, then he fires me."

"Hey, this is a good song," Jim said, abruptly pulling Irene from her seat. "Let's dance."

"Did you catch trouble from Theo, too?" Britt asked Artemios.

"No, not me. Theo barks, but me he does not bite."
Artemios tugged on a set of gold chains around his neck that
dipped inside his blue shirt, open halfway down his chest.

"So how long have you worked for Theo?"

"Since the Alevras family bought the winery. That was in
'79. Theo's papa owns a vineyard on Crete. Theo runs the
winery here on Santorini."

"Why did they build the winery here instead of on Crete?"

"They didn't build. The winery has been here many years.
Thirty years, maybe forty. Bottled only a hundred cases a
year. Now we do over two thousand in a good year."

"So you brought in grapes from the Crescent Vineyard
after the expansion?"

"That is right." Artemios became still. "Why do you ask
so many questions?"

"I like to know about things."

"I like to dance." Artemios plucked Cassie's sleeve.
"Come, let's go."

After Cassie and Artemios left the table, Britt turned to
the young Kazantas. "What will you do for a job now?" she
asked.

Irene's brother narrowed his black eyes, then reached into
his shirt pocket for cigarettes. Once ignited, the Turkish
tobacco burned with a bitter odor that mingled with the larger
currents of body odors and liquor. Georgios's eyes would not
move from his sister, swaying on the dance floor with her
husband–to–be. Britt swiveled around to watch the square
packed with beat–driven bodies. She focused on Cassie,
bobbing to the music. Her silver bracelets flashed in the
lights. Her billowing white shirt, tucked into tight jeans,
glowed with a violet hue.

I'm not having fun, Britt said to herself. I'm definitely not
having fun, she repeated when the foursome stayed on the
floor for another dance. As she watched Artemios lean toward

Cassie, put his hands on her shoulders, bend to her ear, Britt's breathing constricted. Reality check, she told herself. The lady's straight. For the first time in her life, Britt found herself longing for Nicki's companionship. Why can't I just fall in love with her and be done with it, she thought?

Artemios seemed to be engaged in a playful sort of pleading. He opened his arms to Cassie. He covered his heart with his hands. When at last she held up hers in reproach, he slid one of the gold chains from his neck and dropped it over Cassie's head. She jabbed a finger toward him, as if in rebuke.

When the beat bled into a new song, Cassie and Artemios returned to the table. Britt heard a couple of beeps when the young Greek swung past her.

"Sorry to be gone so long," Cassie said, her face glistening with sweat. "I didn't know that last cut would go on forever."

Her dance partner removed a pager from his belt and shut it off. "I must go," he said. "The boss calls."

"We saw the *Praxis* offshore a little while ago," Britt shouted over the music. "Are you going there?"

"Not to it. I go pick up some cargo."

"Really? At this time of night?"

Artemios shrugged. "We must have bottles to put wine into. Otherwise we drink from the barrels." He laughed at his joke.

When Britt turned to Cassie for her reaction to Artemios's leaving, she found her talking to a young German with a heavy accent. "Come," he said. "Just one."

"One more," Cassie said to Britt as she left for the dance floor.

Relegated once again to the role of watcher, Britt began to lose her enthusiasm for the computer programmer. Instead, she eyeballed Theo's hired hand, Artemios, as he squeezed his way through the surging crowd. I could use some air, Britt said to herself, latching on to an excuse to leave. But air had nothing to do with it. In her heart, she knew that she didn't want to watch Cassie dancing with others when what she wanted was to dance with her herself. But what on earth did I expect? Britt thought. Cassie is a straight lady in a straight bar. Britt quickly slipped through the steaming throng to the exit.

The sea air slapped Britt full in the face as it rushed through the intersections of the village. Britt gasped at its freshness, then stepped off the veranda on to the road. She struggled to put Cassie out of her mind. In the distance, Artemios sauntered across the sand to a boat bobbing next to a small cement landing. He caught the line thrown to him, then secured the craft.

As Britt watched, Theo's men unloaded crates of about a cubic yard each. She moved unconsciously toward the beach for a better view. That's an odd size for empty bottles to be shipped in, she said to herself. And given the way that the men struggled with the crates, they certainly held something heavier than empty bottles.

She saw a pickup truck back onto the landing. The driver jumped out and began helping load the freight into the back. He and Artemios lifted the crates together, one by one, out of the arms of the sailors in the boat and laid them in the bed of the truck.

Artemios slid into the passenger's seat when the last of the six crates thudded into place and the tailgate was secured. The driver revved the engine, while the boat glided from the landing and headed back to the yacht.

To Britt's consternation, the small Datsun drove straight ahead on the road running past the disco. She slipped back into the shadows of a building, hoping that Artemios had not seen her as the truck rumbled by. Watching the tail lights veer toward the Fira Winery, Britt wondered what the crates really contained.

It was then, moved by curiosity and a desire to put significant distance between her and the disappointments within the disco, that Britt made an impulsive decision. She decided to follow.

12

Britt untangled her Vespa from the row of scooters and mopeds by the disco and climbed aboard. On the third kick, the engine coughed to life for a moment, then died.

"Damn," she snapped. As she lifted herself on her toes, ready to slam the start pedal with her entire one–hundred–and–twenty–five pounds, a voice rang out.

"Ditching me?" Cassie appeared next to Britt, her hands on her slim hips.

"No," Britt said, fidgeting with the clutch. "I wanted a night ride. I'll be back."

"Revenge for my abandoning you at the table?"

"You don't need my permission to dance."

Cassie didn't say anything. She just kept her eyes fixed on Britt.

"I did feel pretty damn awkward sitting all alone with Georgios."

Cassie placed a hand on Britt's shoulder. "Sorry. I should have been more sensitive."

Britt's anger flamed out. "You're not responsible for my entertainment, Cass. Let's not make a big deal out of it, okay?"

"Deal." Cassie eyed the Vespa. "So, where are you going?"

"Oh, down the road a ways."

"You know, you wouldn't need to stop back for me if you take me along."

"True."

"Maybe we could stop at the Fira Winery," Cassie said, sliding her hand to Britt's far shoulder. "Artemios insisted that I wear one of his necklaces for the night. He forgot to take it when he left. If I keep it overnight, he'll probably claim we're engaged."

"Perfect," Britt grinned. The Vespa jumped to life with one kick.

Cassie threw her leg over the seat and snuggled in close.

The scooter sputtered past a row of barrel vaulted buildings, then rose into a smooth purr when the gears jumped into third. The small headlight of the two–wheeler threw a pathetic beam along the deserted road lined by eucalyptus trees. The pungent breeze slapped the women and made their teeth chatter. As they flew along the road, Britt decided that she liked Cassie's hands on her waist. When she sensed Cassie's grip tighten, she experienced a rush of pleasure and a loose grin pasting itself on her face.

They tilted into a curve and slowed to make the sharp right turn into the Fira Winery.

"The gate's open," Cassie cried.

They tore up the narrow lane toward the yellow lights of the winery, which were blazing like candles in the pitch dark. The trucks they had seen at the Athinios harbor several days earlier formed a haphazard row on the south side. Artemios's pickup was not in sight.

Britt guided the Vespa over the ground, baked as hard as concrete. Just as the women rounded the corner of the small, squat building, three figures dashed from a side door. Two of them carried what appeared at first to be blunt sticks. Britt pressed into the handlebars as she flew past them, then angled to the rear of the winery. She wheeled around at the truck that had picked up the crates at Kamari Beach. It was backed up to the loading dock; its the bed was empty. Under the yawning hood two men worked on the engine.

"Where's Artemios?" Britt shouted above the idling engine.

The guards they had passed at the side of the building came up behind them. Britt circled around to face them. The AK–47s in the men's hands drooped slightly.

"No need for those," Britt said, keeping her voice firm and steady. "We came for Artemios. Where is he?"

The mechanics joined ranks with the guards and broke into a jagged exchange with them. Dressed in jeans and grease–stained T–shirts, they shrugged at the women. Britt could pick out the word "American."

"You want Artemios?" one of them asked. He had short brown hair and a missing front tooth.

Britt and Cassie nodded.

He curved a couple of fingers into his mouth and whistled shrilly into the winery. "Artemios! Artemios!" he yelled across the loading dock.

Britt craned her neck to see into the building. Sawdust covered the floor. A hydraulic elevator was on one side of the opening. In the back a dozen wooden barrels rested on their sides. Britt estimated them to be at least eight feet in diameter. Wedges of wood, like doorstops, kept the barrels in place. Wine presses, stained purple with the blood of the trade, stood in a far corner. A rich, musty smell permeated the evening air.

Artemios, backlit against the bright lights, loped toward the loading dock, wiping his brow with a handkerchief. When he saw the Americans, he turned ashen.

"What are you doing?" he shouted. "You go! You go now!"

"Hey," Cassie said, "you forgot to take your chain back." She pulled it off her neck and tossed it at him. The gold snaked lazily through the air.

"I forgot. Yes." Artemios snatched the necklace before it hit the concrete floor. "You should not have come. You go. Now."

"All right," Britt said, revving the engine to a whinny. "Tell Theo hello from us."

"See you!" Cassie cried as Britt stomped on the gas. The Vespa lurched forward and sailed from the Fira Winery.

Halfway between the winery and Kamari, Britt geared down and eased the scooter to the side of the road. Placing one foot on the ground, she came to a complete stop, then killed the light.

Cassie jumped off the back. "Holy god," she said, peering at the glow from the winery, "what's going on there?"

Britt creaked her leg over the spine of the scooter. "You've lived here for a year and a half. You tell me."

"I don't know," Cassie said. Her face glowed with a pale blue in the moon's light. "I've never seen guns on the island. Even the police up in Thera don't carry weapons."

"Those were more than guns," Britt said. "AK–47s are death machines. Must be vintage wine they're protecting."

"Hardly. It's Lysol with a buzz."

Britt paced around the scooter, never taking her eyes from the steady glare of lights in the distance. "Then what are they protecting?"

"Or who? Theo keeps some Neanderthals around him. Bodyguards, I've always assumed."

"Why does he need bodyguards?"

"I always thought for his ego." Cassie watched Britt move panther–like through the darkness.

"Hmmm," Britt sounded. "Did you notice something peculiar about those cartons sitting by the elevator?"

"Can't say that I did. I kept my eyes on the guns."

"I think they were the crates taken off the ferry at Athinios yesterday—they had the same logo as on the truck. Artemios told me they were bringing in grapes from the Crescent Vineyard on Crete. The crates were still nailed shut. Nobody seemed particularly concerned that they weren't refrigerated. Plus, they're much deeper than normal crates used to ship grapes, unless they do things differently here in Greece than they do in California. I visited a few wineries in Napa Valley when I was in grad school."

"Want to go back for another peek?"

"Great idea, Cass." Britt's laugh was low and rich. "I'd rather do it in the daylight, with a certified tour guide—one who has a gun permit." Britt climbed aboard the Vespa.

"You mean the police?" Cassie asked, her voice tightening.

"No. I don't know what I mean. Let's call it a night and not say anything to anyone about it."

"We can try to forget about it, but I doubt those guys at the winery will." Cassie said, fitting herself behind the professor.

Silently, Britt agreed. Their visit may have stirred up the hive. This was something Rich Marcello should hear about. To her surprise, Britt found herself anticipating the conversation with more relief than apprehension.

In a few minutes, they rolled through the main drag of Kamari, then rounded the road pointed east that was lined with hotels and pensions. As Britt came to a stop in front of Cassie's pension, she regretted the end of the ride, and Cassie taking her hands from her waist.

"Come in for a drink," Cassie said, slipping off the back end.

"Just what I need," Britt said, tapping down the kickstand.

"What do you need?" a deep voice asked.

The women spun around. Stepping from the circle of veranda lights was Bob Collins, grinning like a bridegroom.

13

"Where did you come from?" Cassie cried.

"From Athens," Bob said, crunching across the gravel. "On an evening flight."

"How long have you been here?"

"A while. Maria said she thought you were down at the beach or at the disco. I checked both. I found Jim nearly passed out at the Volcano. He said you guys had been at the disco, but then split. I thought it best to come back and wait. I'm having some Retsina. Want some?"

Britt glanced at Cassie. "Thanks, Bob. I was just saying I could use a drink." She hoped that her accepting the offer would mask her disappointment at the way the evening had turned out.

"What have you been up to?" he asked, taking in their flushed faces.

"Riding the back roads," Britt said quickly, clueing Cassie to how tightly she wanted the secret held about the incident at Fira Winery. "It got a bit chilly."

A couple of sofas delineated a small square of a lounge area immediately inside the front door. A glass with a thin pool of yellow liquid sat in the middle of a marble coffee table.

"Have a seat," Bob said, plopping on the center cushion of a sofa. Britt placed herself at right angles to him on the other couch, and Cassie slumped into a matching chair.

"So, what are you doing here?" Cassie asked.

"I thought I'd surprise you," Bob said. His hair glowed like maple syrup under the illumination of a floor lamp.

"You did."

The black skirt of Maria Bountourakis swished between
the furniture. The widow clinked two glasses on the table.
"Drink?" she asked, holding up the bottle of Retsina.
"Thanks, Maria," Britt said, after the proprietor filled the
glasses. "Would you like to join us?"
"You are good to ask," she replied in a soft voice. "Not
tonight, okay? You want me to leave the bottle?"
"Yes," Bob said.
"No," Cassie said. "Take it with you."
Maria nodded and floated from the circle, bottle in hand.
Britt sipped her drink and savored the bite of the turpentine-
flavored alcohol on the back of her tongue.
"I thought you were going to take school more seriously
this summer," Cassie said, her eyebrows scrunched together.
"I am. I think about it all the time."
"You said you'd study in earnest instead of playing.
Sounds like you're island hopping again. Just how many
classes are you taking?"
"One," Bob said sheepishly.
"Why don't you quit pretending you're a scholar?"
"There's nothing wrong with part–time students, is there
Professor Evans?" Bob turned his large, deep–set eyes on
Britt.
She bent her mouth upward in what she hoped looked like
a genuine smile. "Full–time is best for a scholar. But few
people are the genuine issue."
"I'm strictly a student, thank you. No desire to be single–
minded." Bob rubbed his short brown beard. "I'm a dilet-
tante. I dabble in the arts, in history, in the sun."
Cassie frowned. "I'd like to see you put that on a resume."
Bob showed a row of even, white teeth. "I don't need a
resume, thank god. I can be an excavation bum for the rest of
my life. A little Akrotiri, a little Corinth, a little Heraklion, a
little..."

"Just how do you support yourself, if you don't mind my asking?" Britt asked, luring Bob's eyes away from Cassie.

"Not at all. I live off the fat of the land."

"Meaning the fat of his parent's trust." Cassie set her glass back on the table.

"Ah–ha!" Britt opened her mouth in a not quite real yawn. "I'm finished for the night. Thanks for the drink, Bob." She turned to the programmer. "Thanks for tonight, Cass. I had fun—most of the time." Britt flashed a smile, then was gone.

"Time to hit the hay," Bob said, once the door had closed behind Britt.

"Did you get a room here?"

"Uh, no. I thought we'd share, as usual."

"It's not usual any more, Bob. You know that."

"I can't get a room here. I'm sure Maria is booked solid— it's summer, for Christsakes. She let me put my stuff in your place. She expects me to stay with you."

"I don't give a damn about other people's expectations." Cassie sighed. "Come on. I'll set you up in my room since you've claimed it already."

Bob padded after Cassie to her room. She found the slapping of his sandals against his heels annoying. She remembered when she had thought the sound endearing.

"Didn't we agree not to see each other for a while?" Cassie sat in her desk chair, facing Bob who belly flopped across the bed. Except for the pictures, which were of Greek landscapes, and a small refrigerator and hot plate, the room was a replica of Britt's.

"No, we didn't agree to that. You told me that's what you wanted."

Cassie stared out the French doors at the windows of Britt's room across the small grove of spindly pistachio trees.

She saw the lights snap on in her room. "So, why can't you respect my wishes?"

"Cassie," Bob replied in hushed tones, "you haven't given us a chance."

"The time for chances," Cassie said, getting up and drawing closed the drapes, "is over."

"Jesus, can't you relax?" Bob said, thumping a pillow into the headboard, then sitting up against it. "Can't we just have a good time this weekend? Lie on the beach. Eat. Drink. I don't want anything else. Just your company."

"That's hard for me to believe." Cassie returned to her chair.

"Believe." Bob flattened his mustache with a finger. "I'm not asking for a commitment, just friendship. Just more time."

"Your time is over," Cassie said firmly.

"That's not fair. It's not like I'm trying to bug you. I haven't seen you since—"

"—since Bounty's funeral. That wasn't so long ago."

"Well, it's not as though I've been on your doorstep every moment."

"No. But give me some peace, will you?"

"How much?" Bob smiled impishly.

"You can shove that dumb grin of yours, too."

Bob steadied his brown eyes on Cassie's face. "So, are you getting it on the side?"

"That doesn't even deserve an answer."

He shrugged. "I just have to know where I stand."

"I'm not involved with anyone."

"A late-night ride with the Professor. She certainly had a good time. Sounds suspicious to me."

"You know, you're really pissing me off."

"Am I? Word at the school is that she likes the ladies."

Cassie's eyes narrowed. "If that's news to you, where have you been?"

"That doesn't bother you, then?"

"You're the one who seems worked up about it."

Bob gestured gently for Cassie to join him, his eyes soft. "I thought you might need a little support in case you're confused."

"Bob, just leave me alone."

"Listen. Britt's queer. I don't want you messing around with her."

"If you're that worried, where were you when she first came?"

Bob's eyes hardened slightly. "I didn't think I had anything to worry about. Then I never heard from you. Even after the letter. You should have called."

"I didn't want to."

"Well, I got worried."

"Or dumped by your current squeeze?"

"That's not fair."

"No, it's not," Cassie said, triumphant. "You mess up your latest conquest, and you're on the next plane to me. I'm touched."

"It's not like that. Not at all. It just took my going out with someone else to figure out how much it's you I really want."

"You can't have me."

"It's worth another try. Christ, don't leave me for some dyke."

"I left you before I met Britt."

"But you're sleeping with her, aren't you?"

"You're drunk. It's never come up between us. She's never even discussed her love life."

He wagged his head. "You're dreaming. She's gonna put the moves on you, wait and see. Sooner or later, it's gonna happen."

"Then I hope it's sooner rather than later," Cassie said, snatching the current issue of *Newsweek* from her desk and heading for the door, "and I'll send you a wedding invitation."

"Where are you going?"

"Maria's," Cassie said, slamming the door behind her.

"You know, your Bob, he is a good boy," Maria said, patting down the sheets on her living room sofa. "Do not be so hasty to do away with him. Sometimes you do not think someone is so important until they are gone."

"I know," Cassie said, shaking a pillow into its case, "and I appreciate what you're going through, losing..."

The Greek woman swiped the air with a dark, broad hand. "I speak of Bob, not Paulos. Bob cares for you. Otherwise he would not come so far to see you."

"He doesn't love me. I know I don't love him. That's what's important." She idly took in her room for the night, a tastefully furnished area with stuffed, damask chairs to match the couch, and white walls with only a couple of religious reproductions. An oak credenza, which straddled the boundary shared by the living room and dining room, fielded a regiment of framed photographs of several generations of the family.

"Not always. Paulos and me, we were not as close as many husbands and wives. We had no children. But he was better than no husband, even though it was not love like in the movies. We were good for each other."

"You seemed to be," Cassie said, dropping onto the make-shift bed, her arms around the pillow. "I miss him."

Maria, standing over Cassie, plucked lint from her black skirt. "Many people do. I, I just tell myself sometimes that he is away on one of his trips. I know that is not a good thing to do, but it helps me now. Now, for you, you sleep and perhaps in the morning, things look different."

After the proprietor left, Cassie thumbed the magazine to the lead story about the most recently failed Middle Eastern peace talks. She read the same paragraph five times, then tossed the weekly aside.

Of course, Bob was right. She was confused, but she'd never admit it. Not to him. Not to Britt.

I am enchanted, Cassie thought. I don't think it's sexual, though. It's the thrill of having found a good friend on this godforsaken island. But, she admitted, it was more than that. She had heard the whispers at the school in Athens and had found herself anticipating Britt's stay on Santorini. She never really analyzed why, settling instead for the superficial reason of meeting someone different, even exotic. But now she wondered if that had been the real reason. She was aware that she had become quite fond of Britt. She even felt a bit protective of her in an odd sort of way, sensing a vulnerability that Britt tried hard to cover. She thought of the experience at the disco and how she had sensed Britt watching her, then ignoring her. All the while she was dancing, she was wondering what Britt was thinking. Every moment with her seemed sharp and complex.

"I've got to stop thinking about her," Cassie said out loud, snapping off the light and turning toward a long, restless night.

14

"Lady Luck may have just shaken her wand at us," Rich Marcello said the next day. His voice was shot through with static. "Greek wineries don't post guards, and the government isn't keen on an armed citizenry. I'd bet my security clearance those weapons were contraband. Good work, Britt."

The professor cupped her hand over the mouth piece of the phone as the pension's cleaning woman passed the front desk. "Thanks. So you'll check into it?"

"You bet. I'll put some diggers on it first thing Monday a.m. The Fira Winery on Santorini and the Crescent Vineyard on Crete."

"Right. Both owned by the Alevras family."

"Juicy," Marcello said. "At last we have something to hang on to. Good for us, but I don't want you coming up a loser on this one."

"Think I'm in trouble?"

"Maybe. This Alevras guy will know you've been scouting out his shop. He might not want to risk hurting you, though, if there's a connection to the Bountourakis incident."

"I agree. In fact, a few days ago Theo slapped some kid around because he almost beaned me while unloading cargo."

"Hold on, partner," Marcello said. "Take a step back. What happened?"

Britt recounted the incident of the swinging crate at the Athinios harbor. "I'm sure it was an accident," she concluded.

"I'm not so sure," Marcello said. "Who was the kid?"

"Georgios Kazantas," Britt said, "the younger brother of a woman engaged to one of the Akrotiri crew."

"Incestuous lot down there. No Kazantas appeared on Bounty's police reports, so that's another thread worth pulling."

"Was Theo Alevras questioned concerning the death of Bounty?"

"Yep. General stuff—the authorities considered him pretty much of a hanger–on with the Akrotiri crew, if I recall. Maybe he wasn't asked the right questions."

"I wouldn't be surprised. The family's prominent."

"Then they may have glossed over this one. Anything else?"

"Not now."

"You've given me a fistful, lady." Marcello paused. "I don't want to sound ungrateful, but why? When I last spoke with you, I thought you'd sooner twist my head off than pass along any dirt you'd dig up."

Britt sighed loudly. "I was hoping you wouldn't ask me that."

"Was it my charm that finally sunk in?"

"No, something much more self–serving—personal safety. Those weapons at the winery told me that I might be dealing with some heavyweights. If that's the case, I want you and your cavalry on my side the moment I call for help."

"Pretty keen instinct for survival, I'd say. Listen, Britt, you'll be in Athens next weekend, won't you?"

"Attending a symposium. That's the plan."

"How about meeting Sunday morning. By then I should have a nice chunk of inside dope on these guys."

"Terrific. Public phones aren't the best way to talk about this."

"Agreed. Embassy. Ten o'clock."

"How about something closer to home this time? Say Kolonaki Square?"

"Name the spot." Marcello paused again. "One more thing. Stick to your research this week. No poking this mess with a stick. Even a long one. Not 'til we know that this Alevras guy is benign. Frankly, I doubt he is. Let's not fool around with him. I don't want some front–end loader digging you out of the ash mines."

An hour later, Britt parked her Vespa at the cul–de–sac on Mesa Vouno that served both as a terminus and a parking lot. A few scooters, a couple of taxis and four donkeys with their owners filled the circle of pavement. Britt, playing the role of tourist at this archaeological site, held out a handful of drachmas to the guard at the gate, then proceeded up the winding path toward the Classical ruins.

A little over halfway there, she passed the stone carvings of the lion, the dolphin, and the eagle. Resting a hand on the stone with Zeus's bird, Britt adjusted her daypack and enjoyed the expanse of sea and land far below.

At the site, Britt picked her way along the foot paths snaking through acres of broken stones. Unlike the Minoan ruins at Akrotiri, which came from the fourteenth century B.C., these ruins dated from the third century B.C. At the summit of the second highest mountain on the island, the site afforded a bird's–eye view of the land and surrounding sea. To the northeast, Britt counted nine small islands, and to the south, Crete appeared as a smudge on the hazy seam of the horizon, more mirage than reality. The highest mountain, Prophetus Elias, loomed next door, blocking a view of the western side of the island. A monastery and NATO radar station perched on its summit.

A trespasser in the once men–only city, Britt wandered through the ruins, some parts still decorated with ancient graffiti of male genitals. Black beetles the size of nickels trundled across the paths, and hordes of ants marched in ever changing directions. The burnt grass and dried thistles along the path rustled with the quick movement of small gray lizards. After nearly an hour in the merciless sun, Britt sought respite from the heat in a cluster of pines northeast of the theater. She pulled out a small bottle of water from her backpack, drank, then sat quietly, listening to the furious buzz of huge black flies.

Hot and satisfied, she started back to the parking lot. Just before she reached the stone carvings of the animals, Britt strayed from the beaten path to an outcropping that afforded the most spectacular view of the island. The entire crescent of land lay before her. Small groups of buildings marked the island villages, and a patchwork of odd-shaped fields filled the spaces between the settlements. Tiny monasteries popped up everywhere like alabaster mushrooms against the gray land, their domes painted blue to symbolize the sky.

Britt sat on a rock and concentrated on the stretch of Kamari Beach some twelve hundred feet below her. At least a hundred sun bathers dotted the black surface like grains of tossed rice. Britt picked out Cassie's pension from the cluster of buildings inland from the beach. She quickly turned her attention back to the strip of sand, shutting out thoughts of Cassie and Bob and what they might be doing. She was surprised at her jealousy and alarmed at the feelings underlying it. That she could allow herself to fall for Cassie was...well, preposterous. She absolutely would not permit it.

To the north, a couple of fishing boats were moored at the concrete landing where the motor boat had put ashore last night. Britt traced the road Artemios had taken to the Fira Winery, through the northern streets of Kamari, past the disco and barrel–vaulted homes, past dusty fields of grapes and tomatoes.

Thirsty again, Britt rummaged in her pack for the bottle of mineral water. Hunched over at an odd angle to the ground, she caught a flash of green wedged between two rocks.

"No photos," a voice warned, coming from the path.

Slipping the bottle from her pack, Britt swung around to find the source of the command. A guard, his face cracked from years in the sun, held up a finger to her, then pointed at the airport in the distance.

Britt swatted at a fly, then focused on the island's airport, which was owned by the military. It sported the largest field on Santorini—the concrete runway. A tiny monastery blossomed in the rocks near the tarmac at the northeastern corner. The American shook her head at the guard. "No photos," she repeated, and the guard plodded on, clinking his worry beads.

Alone once again, Britt bent down and extracted from a small crevice an empty box of Fuji film. No photos. Sure thing. Somebody had been up here shooting—or at least changing film. The box said ISO 1600, a speed that only a pro would use. Why use such a fast film here? she asked herself. Action shots? The only action at this height was the wind. Night shots? Of what? Britt inspected the box more closely. On one side, she saw Πβ scratched into the box. "Pi and beta," Britt muttered. "PB. Paulos Bountourakis."

Britt's spine stiffened. Could this be where Bounty had been shooting the night of his death? He told Cassie he was going to take pictures of Kamari Beach. There it was, stretched like a black ribbon far below, and in the background the airport. Cassie said he'd taken his car that night—two blocks to a place where he probably couldn't find a spot to park. It didn't make sense. Instead of going to the beach, had he made the turnoff to Mesa Vouno and come here, right to this spot?

The wind rose to a wail. Britt spun around and stared into the eyes of the stone eagle.

"What did you see?" she demanded. Her flesh rose in goosebumps as the wails continued, sounding around the open beak of the granite bird. "What did you see?"

Again, Britt looked out across the island, trying to imagine what had transpired just a few weeks previously. Failing in that effort, and eager to leave the dizzying heights and the profound alarm she felt, Britt tossed the water bottle and film box into her pack. As she turned to go, she saw a pair of expensive Italian shoes next to her. She looked up, expecting to see the crinkled face of another guard. Instead, standing above her, arms folded across his chest, was Theo Alevras.

"Why did you come to the winery last night?" he hissed. His eyes, hard as onyx, bore into the professor. He had on designer jeans and a polo shirt with a tiny reptile stitched to its front.

"Cassie and I needed to return something to Artemios," Britt said, rising to her feet. She angled her body toward the Greek so that she could keep sight of the drop off less than a yard away.

Alevras waved a hand in the air. "The gold chain. That was an excuse, not a reason. I ask you again, why did you come to the winery last night?"

Britt studied the young owner for a moment. Had he seen her find the film box? Had he seen her put it in her pack? Emboldened by the fact that he had not once looked at it, she decided to be defiant. "Well, then, that's my excuse. Now let me pass."

Alevras moved a leg slightly to reaffirm his position. "Cassie knows that the winery is closed to tourists and islanders who do no business with us. Why did you come?"

"Why did your men wave those guns in our faces?"

"Guns? You are mistaken. Perhaps you saw the batons my guards use. There have been thefts in the past. I must protect my property."

"Thefts? Have you reported them to the police?"

"Do not concern yourself with my affairs, Professor Evans. I could make things very bad for you. Foreigners trespassing on Greek property. Very serious."

"Then I suggest we discuss the whole incident with the police."

"You made a mistake this time," Alevras said, his lips curling. "If there is another time, then I call the police."

"You do that, Theo. If you don't step out of my way now, I'm calling for the guards. Now. There won't be a next time for me."

"Go, then," he said, moving off the path, "but you be careful, Professor. I am watching you."

From his perch, Alevras watched Britt navigate the hairpin turns down the mountain. Down and down she went, sputtering past the stone barriers holding the rocks and earth back from the road, weaving past piles of donkey dung. She had been very foolish last night, he thought, riding out to the winery. Yet it was so brazen, so open, he wondered if she was truly working for Mikos Zerakis—or American intelligence. And what was Cassie doing with her? He slowly tramped back to the parking area, where an old man in a brocade vest tended two sweating donkeys.

Somewhere in his organization was a double dealer, Alevras thought. He had not told his father about the episode of the Americans visiting the winery. But this morning his father, irate as usual, had awakened him with a call. He still insisted that the professor was an agent. She had been asking too many questions at the Athinios dock. Alevras was to make sure she didn't ask any more. He would, if and when he felt like it. He was in control, after all. Couldn't he have killed the American just now? His chance would come, and present itself in such a way that no one would suspect him or anyone associated with the Fira Winery.

15

"You're not quitting, are you?" Cassie sauntered up to Britt on the veranda of the Pelican Restaurant.

"Siesta time," Britt said. She tightened her grip around an Orangina, then raised it to her lips. "I may hit the surf later."

"Why wait? The wind's great! The waves are perfect for a change! Come on, let's catch some tubes!"

"What about Bob?"

"What about him?" Cassie flicked a hand at her ex–boyfriend, stretched in the sun like a curing hide, oblivious to the world. "He'll be fine. Come on, we can do Perissa Beach."

Side by side, the women cut through the dark water on a strong westerly wind, Cassie on her brilliantly colored sailboard, and Britt on her lavender and black rental unit. The wave action was strong, but the two women sliced through the rolls cleanly, their boards singing. Two small fins broke the surface of the water as the women reached the tip of the promontory.

"Company!" Cassie cried, gaining a small lead to the inside. A pair of dolphins leapt through the waves as if on cue.

As the humans angled toward the bulge of land, the water mammals effortlessly dipped in and out of the swelling sea. When Britt and Cassie approached the beach of Perissa, their companions broke away with a flurry of chirps, then split toward the open waters. The women dropped their sails close to shore.

"Quite an escort!" Britt exclaimed as they waded to the beach.

"Great, huh? They follow me around sometimes. I call them Burt and Martha. They must have wanted to check you out." They settled in the shade of a stand of eucalyptus trees. Cassie peeled an orange she had brought along in a mesh bag tied to her sailboard. They each took a section and savored the fruit's sharp, sweet taste.

"So, how's it going with Bob?" Britt asked. Her dark eyes skimmed the horizon.

"All right, I guess." Cassie leaned over the sand to let the juice dribble down. "I'm sorry about his showing up like he did."

"It's not your fault."

"Well, I didn't want the evening to end like that."

Britt propped herself on an elbow and faced Cassie. "How did you want it to end?"

"Talking with you, not him."

"That would have been nice."

"You weren't far from our thoughts. We talked a lot about you."

"Did you?" Britt reached for another orange slice.

"Yeah. He's concerned that you're going to seduce me."

Britt broke into a surprised laugh. "How gallant of him to come to your rescue! What did you do?"

"Stormed out of the room."

"Sounds melodramatic."

"Not really. I slept on Maria's couch," Cassie reported, shifting her eyes toward Britt.

"Ah."

For a while they were quiet, content to absorb the pleasant sensations of the beach: the sound of the beating surf, the urgent cry of hungry gulls, the smell of coconut sunscreen mingling with eucalyptus, the feel of the coarse, black sand, the awareness of each other.

"You don't talk much about your love life, do you?" Cassie said at last.

"Probably because I don't have one." Britt fingered an orange peel, then placed it in Cassie's mesh bag.

"Nursing a broken heart?"

"Not any more."

"Tell me about your last relationship." Cassie bit into the final orange slice.

"There's not much to say. We were together about six months. It ended badly."

"What happened."

"She was straight."

Cassie stopped chewing.

"Before the divorce was finalized," Britt continued, digging her heels in the sand and squinting at the cumulus clouds hanging low in the eastern sky, "she went back to her husband. I didn't even know they had started seeing each other again."

"Ouch."

"It was more like 'Yeee–owww!' for about three months," Britt chuckled sadly. "But that's all behind me. Lesson learned."

Britt felt Cassie examining her, but she would not make eye contact.

"What lesson is that?"

"That I need to be smarter about relationships. I've got to have my mind pumping as well as my heart. I won't step into a situation where I know I'm going to get hurt. I won't be someone's ego trip or sexual adventure."

"I don't blame you." Cassie paused. "So do you have any prospects?"

Britt's cheeks reddened. If circumstances had been different—if Cassie had been different—she might have said 'you.' But knowing Cassie's lifestyle, she refused to accept that what she felt for Cassie was anything more than the commaderie of two American women on an isolated island.

"Am I getting too personal?" Cassie asked.

"Oh, no, no. I have no prospects." Britt stretched out her arms and fixed her sight once more on the sea. When she looked again at Cassie, she found Cassie's eyes holding her own, their expression open and far too deep. Unable to bear the possibilities, Britt scrambled for her windsurfer. "Race you back!" she cried as she ran toward the water.

Cassie darted after Britt. Once on her board, she quickly closed the gap, then passed the professor, her eyes bright with the challenge. As she rounded the tip of the promontory, Britt lagged only a few yards behind.

The piercing whine of an engine broke their competition. From behind the massive tongue of rock, a hydrofoil tore across the open sea. The driver, who had a fisherman's cap pulled low across his forehead, gunned the motor to full power. Before either Cassie or Britt could react, the vehicle, its blade spinning like a fan, ripped the water between them.

The women toppled into the sea. As the water craft disappeared down the coast in a descending drone, Britt surfaced. Cassie did not.

Britt plunged toward Cassie's board, then dove underwater, twisting in every direction, her eyes open in the cold brine. In that moment, suspended in a dark environment, searching for the one she had lost, Britt felt an intense loneliness as horrible as she had ever experienced. God no! God no! her mind cried. Britt felt the world closing down just as a hand grabbed her leg. Cassie rose beside her, steady as a balloon. Together they broke the surface.

"Shit!" Cassie sputtered. "What the hell was that?" She held Britt by the shoulders, squinting at her face.

"A hydrofoil."

"Scared the hell out of me. Are you okay?"

"Now that I know you are." Britt bobbed in the water. She put her hands on Cassie's waist. "You were down a long time."

"Probably not as long as it seemed. I took a major header off the board. I must've sunk halfways to the bottom." Cassie coughed out some of water. "The damn jerk. My goggles got knocked off, too." She gasped for another breath. "And I've lost my contacts."

The women held each other loosely for another minute, giving themselves room to tread water and time to catch their breath. Britt realized then how deeply she had come to care for Cassie. She felt blessed by Cassie's friendship, and wanted more than anything to have it always.

Britt slicked back a patch of Cassie's hair that hung on her forehead. "Ready to head back to shore?" she asked gently.

Cassie nodded and flashed a tentative smile. As she broke from Britt, she gave her a quick kiss on the cheek. "Really," she said, "I'm not so bad for a straight lady." Then she glided toward her sailboard and rolled up on its sleek surface.

Once the women were back on their boards, Theo Alevras lowered his binoculars and hopped to the deck from the poop of the *Praxis*. He sniffed the salty air and shook his tangle of hair in the stiff breeze. He had seen the entire episode. The temptation to jump to the rescue had been almost irresistible. It would have been silly. He was more than three hundred meters from them. Besides, such a mishap would be a fortunate blessing from God. Why interfere?

He leaned on the railing and mulled over the incident. Was this simply an accident that he had witnessed, or had it been a carefully orchestrated attack? If the rundown had been intentional, what was the reason? And who was behind it? His father? Did he no longer trust his son to do a job? If his father had arranged the attack, who was the operative? Theo yelled for a drink. He downed it in one quick swallow, then hurled the glass into the rolling sea.

"Well, it should be reported to someone," Bob said, toweling himself after a swim. "These hydrofoil people can't be zooming around like maniacs. I think we should tell the police in Thera, if nothing else. If they don't care about hurting someone, maybe they'll care about losing tourists. Maybe they'll know who around here owns the hydros."

"I agree," Britt said, running a comb through her wet hair. Her black tangles separated into wavy strands. "We were lucky. The next people may not be as fortunate."

"You can report it if you want," Cassie said. "They'll just tell us that women shouldn't be sailboarding. Or, if we can't resist, we should stay close to shore. They'll find some way to blame the accident on us."

"Why don't we stay here a few more minutes 'til you two settle down. Then, we can drive into Thera, talk to the police, have dinner, a few drinks, and come back."

"Sorry, Bob." Britt began to gather her belongings into a Greenpeace tote bag. "I want to go back to my room now, but dinner sounds good. Why don't you stop by when you're ready?"

"Fine." Bob glanced at Cassie, then spread out on the sand. "I'll see if Jim can come, too."

"Don't bother," Cassie said. "He's on another tear this weekend. He's holding up the wall a few tavernas down." She nodded toward the north end of the beachfront.

Britt dashed across the burning black sand to the beach road. She jumped on the concrete embankment and threaded her way between dozens of mopeds and scooters.

Cassie watched her disappear in a blur of myopia and fought an impulse to run after her. Instead, she stretched out next to Bob for a few more minutes of sun and rest in a futile effort to stop thinking about the dark eyes of the professor.

Sunday evening, Britt knocked softly on the French doors of Cassie's room. Cassie, reading a potboiler on the bed, broke into a grin and motioned her friend inside.

"What are you up to?" Cassie asked.

"I need a break. I've been prepping for this week's research at the museum." Britt stepped across the room. "Nice specs."

"Thanks. I have another pair of contacts, but my eyes are too tired tonight." Cassie slipped a bookmark in her paperback. "So, what's your paper on?"

"'Naturalism in Minoan and Classical Pottery: A Comparative Study.' That's the working title. Later I'll think of an esoteric grabber that will have the publishers drooling."

Britt claimed the desk chair and swept the small room with her eyes. "You put Bob on the plane, I take it."

Cassie nodded. "Dropped him at the airport an hour ago. Thank god he's gone. I decided this weekend that I really don't like him. I think he's lazy, shallow, and rude."

Britt put her feet on the footboard. "He's not that bad, is he?"

"He can be. He almost wrecked my weekend. Thank heaven he can amuse himself when he has too. He spent some time yakking with a couple of fishermen on the beach and picked up a few bits of island folklore."

"Maybe he's in the wrong field. He may be suited more for oral history than archaeology."

"Well, he's wrong for me, that I know," Cassie said.

"Maybe," Britt said, looking out the window. "Listen, I have a favor to ask."

"Name it."

"Do you think you could get me into Bounty's photo lab?"

Cassie sat up. "I could probably get us in. Why?"
"I want to check his camera—and his supply of film."
"Why?"
"I'll tell you when we're in the lab."

16

"So she visits the old man's winery. Big deal." Theo Alevras stared at the red, swollen sun settling on the horizon. Its light spread into the sea like blood. His visitor rearranged himself in a red– and white–striped sling chair. They were aboard the *Praxis* in the Thera harbor.

"It was a big deal when you caught Bountourakis sneaking around the loading dock. Remember?"

Alevras shrugged. "She sees nothing, knows nothing. I have talked to her." The captain dipped his head into a white cotton sweater and stretched it over his bare chest. With the sun nearly below the horizon now, the evening had a sharpening chill. "So, what can she find?"

"Not much, I would think. But who knows? She's bright. She might figure things out. Bountourakis did."

"If he had 'figured things out,' we would be sitting in prison, not on my yacht." A steward appeared out of the darkness and handed the two men each a scotch. "I have talked with her. I am having her watched more closely, too," Alevras said. "I was even watching yesterday afternoon. The incident with the hydrofoil, you know."

"Stupid ass, whoever he was. He could have done us a favor by killing them—or he could have blown up our whole operation in our face. I don't want screwups, especially since we're so close."

"You think I do?" Alevras snorted.

"I didn't say that. I meant we have to be careful."

"Don't worry. You worry too much."

"Three point five million. That's my take. It's worth worrying about."

A low chuckle rumbled from Alevras. "You worry about ten drachmas!"

"I worry because it's my job to worry. I've spent a lot of time setting up the contacts. It either goes perfectly or it doesn't go at all."

Alevras planted his sneakers on the deck and eased himself to his feet. "It will go," he said, stretching his arms in wide circles. "Perfectly. We take care of everybody. Especially ourselves. What can be more simple?"

"That's your trouble. You think everything is easy. Or should be. Let the peons work while you rake in the dough."

"No problem with that?"

No problems, ever, the visitor thought. If something really wasn't a problem, Theo's incompetence would make it one. Like Bountourakis.

"A lot of things, Theo," he said, draining his glass. "More than you'd ever want to imagine. Come on. Let's go below. I want to see the logistics for the transfer."

"You go down, my friend. I join you in a minute."

Alevras strolled the deck alone, his hand running along the varnished mahogany railing. The calm waters of the caldera gently lapped the sideboards, the sound smooth and comforting. High above, the lights of Thera glared harshly into the night. To the west, stretched the vast emptiness of a lonely sea. He could have been a little boy just then, on his grandfather's fishing boat early in the morning, rowing across the black sea as the sun, showing her pink skirts, waited coyly beneath the horizon. They would lay out the lines then, he and his grandfather, rowing a quiet circle. Then, with grunts they'd pull in the net, heavy—or not so heavy—with fish.

At first, he had felt sorry for the fish, flopping around helplessly, their lidless eyes staring at him. But he had grown

accustomed to them. You had to grow accustomed to everything in this world. Otherwise, you could cry your life away.

Now his father would be King Midas with all the wealth
of the Mediterranean, and he the ungrateful heir. Money to
buy anything he'd want. A bigger yacht, one with gold
faucets and platinum toilets. Women and more women.
Alevras chuckled. He was happier when he was a little boy
with nothing in his pockets...and no stallion in his pants.
Well, maybe not. He tipped his cap back on his head and
trotted below deck.

"I have not been in here since the police brought his
equipment back," Maria said, twisting the key in the lock.
The photo lab was at the back of the Bountourakis apartment,
which constituted a small, separate wing of the pension.
"Everything is still in the box. Except the film. The police
kept the two rolls found with him."

"Did they give you the prints?"

Maria shook her head. "No. No exposures. He had not
taken any pictures before the accident." She flicked on the
lights. The room popped into view, revealing an area a bit
bigger than a large walk–in closet. Formica counters ringed
the walls, all with enclosed wood cabinets underneath with
sliding doors. A cardboard box sat on the counter to the right
of the doorway. The legs of a dusty tripod stuck out.

"The darkroom is there," Maria said, pointing to a door
next to a sink. "My husband did not use it much. It takes much
water to develop film, and fresh water on the island is scarce."
The widow ran a finger along a countertop. "Dust. I must
clean the room." Her eyes wandered over the surfaces.
"Sometime. I think I leave you girls here, okay?"

"Sure, Maria," Cassie said. "We'll let you know when
we're done, then you can lock up."

"You will not disturb anything?"

"We'll leave everything as we found it," Britt assured her.

"Okay, what's up?" Cassie said as soon as she closed the door behind Maria.

Britt tossed the Fuji film box on a counter. "That. Could it be Bounty's?"

"His or two hundred tourists."

"Look again," Britt said, opening the refrigerator. Rows of small green boxes appeared.

"Pretty fast film for tourists."

"Exactly. Plus, his initials are scratched on the side."

Cassie turned the box around. "So they are."

Britt slid out a crisper drawer filled with more Kodak and Fuji film. She turned her attention back to the green boxes. "He's got a few rolls of ISO 1600 film." She slipped a box from the end of a row and closed the refrigerator door. "Let's compare the cartons."

"What's to compare?"

"Any price tag?"

"No."

"See any dates or lot numbers?"

"Here. Let's see the one from the 'fridge."

As the women held together the two boxes, one faded and shabby, the other bright and clean, Britt felt Cassie's hand lightly touch hers. Part of her wanted to pull away, but a greater part couldn't resist the magnetic force.

"Same lot numbers."

"Okay," Cassie said, "where'd you find this?"

"On top of Mesa Vouno." Britt leaned back against the counter, breaking contact. For a moment, she wondered if Cassie had felt anything, or if the touch meant as little as Nicki's meant to herself.

"Mesa Vouno?"

"What was Bounty doing taking pictures up there? Was he taking them the night he died? You said he was going to Kamari Beach. Could he have gone up the mountain?"

"I suppose. I didn't watch him drive all the way to the beach. He could have turned off on the road to the mountains. But why?"

"That does seem to be the question. As well as a few others. Like, why did a professional photographer have only two rolls of film on him?"

"He always carried at least five or six."

"Then what happened to the others?"

Cassie set the weather beaten box of film on the counter. "I don't like this, Britt."

"Me either, Cass. I'll talk to a friend of mine in Athens who has government connections. He might have some ideas."

"Well, if his idea is for us to talk to the island police, he'd better think again."

"I'll let him know." A slide projector sitting at the end of the counter caught Britt's attention. She reached over and flicked on the switch. The machine's fan whirred and a small rectangle of color appeared on the wall.

"What's this?" Britt asked as she focused the projector. The slide showed the fresco from Akrotiri called "The Boxing Children" in which sway-backed boys in loincloths were punching at each other. But unlike the cracked and faded fresco, this picture had an unmarred surface laced with vibrant colors.

"Oh," Cassie said, "Bounty and I were playing around with computer graphics outside of work. I haven't paid much attention to it lately. Here, I'll turn off the light so you can see better."

Britt ignored the sudden darkness. "This is gorgeous!" she exclaimed. She clicked on the next slide, "The Fisherman," which showed a solitary man dangling a line of fish.

"Bounty took photographs of a few frescos, then I scanned them into my computer. I manipulated them with a souped up graphics application to 'repair' the damage done to the frescos. Then, Bounty took the computer graphic, captured it, and turned it into a slide."

"You did this?"

"Don't act so surprised. I may be a programmer, but I do have some artistic sense...though some people might consider this as bad as colorizing *Casablanca*. That's my version of how that fresco looked after it first dried on the wall."

Britt snapped through six more slides, then came to the end of the tray. She backed up to look at the last two. One was of a surfer on top of a huge, curling wave. The other a donkey standing outside a souvenir shop with racks of woven blankets and bright handbags. "Yours?"

"Uh–huh. These are just experiments. With the donkey graphic, I wanted to work with complex lines and lots of colors. The surfer picture—which is an old shot of me at Big Sur—gave me a chance to work with blending colors to get practically the entire spectrum of blue. I blocked out all the glare to give it that continuous coloring. I'm still not quite satisfied with how it worked, or how the wave tips turned out. They look weird."

"I think they look delicate," Britt said, peering closely at the cobalt sea curling into a huge tube—the perfect wave— with silver tips scattering into white spray. When Britt stood back up, she found that Cassie had moved closer. "I'm impressed. Is there anything you can't do?"

"Get you to make a pass at me, it seems."

Cassie's eyes had picked up the colors projected on the wall. They appeared luminous and large, with an unmistak-

able look: desire. The mental barriers that Britt had constructed against her passion clattered down into a heap. She
turned into Cassie's arms.

When their lips met softly for a moment, like sheer
curtains fluttering against each other, they did not back away.
Cassie clasped Britt to her, and their kiss grew more impas-
sioned. Their mouths moved in ever broader circles, pressing
harder and deeper. Their breasts touched and their embrace
tightened. Cassie made a small noise.

Suddenly aware of her own ragged breathing, Britt
stepped back, shocked at her loss of control. "I can't do this!"
she cried.

"Please, Britt," Cassie whispered.

"No! No!" Britt fled the small studio, leaving behind two
women, one an image flat and static on the wall, the other
more real and dangerous than she would ever have believed.

17

"You work late tonight," Dr. Gavas exclaimed when he spotted Jim Larson Monday evening at the museum.

Jim's naturally red skin deepened in hue. "Data base maintenance. I want to have everything cleaned up for tomorrow morning. Professor Britt is going on–line." Jim shifted his eyes from Gavas back to the screen. "She wants some special printouts. I thought I'd rig up a routine to pull out the information she needs, then display it in a comprehensible format."

Gavas strolled behind Jim, reading the code on the screen. It meant no more to him than Egyptian hieroglyphics. Jim knew it. Nevertheless, the programmer felt the hair on the nape of his neck rise. The temperature in the small data processing room at the back of the Thera Museum seemed to zoom up ten degrees.

"This computer stuff—it is a mystery to me. I am glad you know what you are doing. Do you think our staff is ready for the reins?"

Jim quickly ran down the list of personnel who would be responsible for data processing and programming. He felt confident in a few of them, and less so with others. He spared Gavas no detail or insight.

"This is a very fine shoulder bag you have," Gavas said, placing a toe against Jim's green daypack resting against a wall. "I look for one like it in the stores."

"It's an old one, from the States," Jim replied, not trusting his voice.

"I go to Germany this fall for a conference. Maybe I will find one there like it." The director of the excavation hoisted the pack off the floor. "These straps have good padding.

Nylon, but anchored to the bag with leather. Very nice. Strong but light." He set the bag back on the floor.

"It's a good one, all right," Jim croaked. "You're not going to Athens for the weekend? You'll be missing the symposium."

"It is unfortunate, but I stay here. My family visits grandparents in the mountains. Weekend after, maybe I go. Maybe one of these years I can afford to have my family stay here with me. The boys, they would not like it, though. Too boring for them."

"Mmmm." Jim entered a string of characters, pressing extra hard on the keyboard. The sound of the clattering keys filled the spartan room. Gavas watched in fascination for several moments as green characters sprang onto the black screen.

"I go then and let you work."

"Okay."

The moment the door closed behind Gavas, Jim snatched his hands from the keyboard. He wiped his full lips with a sweaty palm as the bile of guilt and fear welled up in him. He clambered to the bathroom and heaved until only acid churned in his belly.

"He's been positively surly all day," Cassie complained Tuesday evening as she and Britt examined the stained menu of the Pelican. "You're lucky you were at the museum. We almost threw him into a hole at the site and covered him over. Let the next generation of archaeologists find him."

The three Americans sat at a round table under a low–watt bulb at the back of the taverna. With business light at the early dinner hour, the young owner Andreas had time to show them kabobs of lamb and beef. A white towel hugged his narrow hips.

Britt and Jim both selected souvlaki with pilaf. After a moment of contemplation, Cassie said, "Do you have kota riganati tonight?"

"Just for you," Andreas said, then sauntered into the back room to dish up the chicken flavored with lemon and oregano.

Britt watched Cassie slip the paper menu between a candle holder and a rack of napkins. She thought Cassie the most attractive woman she'd ever met. Her hair was radiant, like a crown of golden wheat, and her smile playful. Then those eyes. When they held her own in a steady gaze, Britt experienced a sharp, twisting, sexual ache.

Sunday night had been a mistake, Britt admitted. While she knew she had fallen in love, she was determined that this was a journey she'd take alone. Cassie would be a heartache down a straight, one–way street.

"Why don't they turn off that tinny noise," Jim complained of the music. "If I wanted wailing, I'd go to that wall in Israel."

"See what I mean?" Cassie said in her rich voice. "He's absolutely impossible."

Given Cassie's complete composure, Britt began to wonder if Sunday night really happened. She turned to Jim. "Is it true?"

"Quite the contrary. I have been my charming self." Jim frowned and reached for the wine bottle to pour himself another glass. His words were heavy and without the usual trace of mockery or humor.

Britt shot Cassie a quizzical look. She, in turn, shrugged her ignorance. Quickly, Britt clapped her hand over Jim's glass. "You're not going to get drunk, Jim. And you are not going to sit around and be unhappy if there's something we can do to help."

Jim clunked the bottle down. He fingered his knife, then the fork, all the while staring at his glass, still capped by a row of female knuckles. He said nothing.

"Jim?" Britt said, moving her hand to his forearm. Her voice was soft and low, but firm.

"Leave me alone."

"Not when I see you constantly drinking yourself into a stupor."

He wagged his head awkwardly as though he had been stunned by a blow to his head.

"Is it Irene?"

He nodded. In the poor light, his red hair took on the color of mud.

"What?"

"You don't understand," he said. "Women make me do foolish things."

Britt burst into laughter. "I do understand. I've done many foolish things for women. But," she continued, "you always have a choice—though your emotions sometimes tell you that you don't. No one *makes* you do anything." She shook his arm gently.

Jim heaved his shoulders, breaking free of contact with Britt. "No more wine for me tonight. That's my choice."

"Are you telling me I'm batting .500?"

"I am."

"All right. That's good enough. For now." She glanced at Cassie, who was watching her closely. "Now, let's have some pita," she said, tearing an end off the pocket bread and dipping it in satsiki sauce.

Later, as the women walked alone up the road to their rooms, Cassie turned to Britt. "I admire how you handled Jim," she said.

"Thanks. I wish I could do more, but that's up to him."

"You've done a lot already."

"I'm concerned about him. He's so unhappy."

"His relationship with Irene is going badly."

"Has he said anything about it to you?"

"No. He's pretty tightlipped. But I do know that the guy has some serious issues. Maybe he thought he could work them out here, away from his family and the American definition of success. Too bad he became entangled in an octopus of a family. There are plenty of good families around. The Kazantas are going to squeeze him for all he's worth."

"Does he realize that?"

"Oh, yeah. He tries not to care about it too much."

They passed a two–story pension under construction. The stark, bright lights in the building's interior revealed the wooden framework amidst swirls of dust. Weary laborers were closing up for the night. A man with a red bandanna tied on his head leaned a board across an open stairwell. With bits of concrete stuck in his heavy mustache, he nodded a greeting to the women, then stooped over to pick up a shovel. The latest Madonna tune rocked in the background.

"I have a question," Cassie said.

"Shoot."

"Your comment tonight at dinner about doing foolish things for women...have there been a lot?"

"Of women? No, not really." Britt laughed. "I won't bother asking you the same question."

"I suppose not." Cassie hesitated. "I've missed you these last two days."

"I guess I've had my nose buried in my research."

"Good. I thought maybe you were avoiding me."

Britt remained silent.

"I have that film box you found," Cassie said. "Why don't you come in and get it. I'll fix us a drink."

"Just take it to work tomorrow. I'll be at the dig in the afternoon."

"No. Come in now." Cassie grinned mischievously. "That shouldn't be a problem since you're not avoiding me."

Britt smiled and slipped her arm through Cassie's. "What a brat," she said as the women headed up the walk.

Cassie popped a few miniature ice cubes into a couple of glasses and gave each a splash of Perrier.

"Here you go," she said, handing the fizzing water to Britt, who had taken the padded chair by the French doors.

Cassie put away the ice tray, then settled at the foot of the bed, legs on the floor, facing Britt. "You know, that was the most exciting kiss I've ever had."

"It didn't exactly put me to sleep either."

"I noticed." Cassie took a sip. "Why did you run away?"

Britt placed both hands around her drink. The ice clinked against the glass. "Because I realized I'd done something pretty stupid. I've fallen in love with you."

"A woman of your intelligence? I'm shocked."

Britt smiled. "I'm sorry. I didn't mean it to sound that way. It's just that I want a relationship that has a chance of working. And you're straight."

"Yes, I have been." Cassie held Britt's eyes. "But I seem to have fallen in love with you too. I want you more than anyone I've ever wanted in my life."

Cassie reached over and placed her drink on the desk next to the faded green Fuji box. To Britt, that flimsy fold of cardboard seemed insignificant now, like a piece in some elaborate boy's game. A smuggling ring on Santorini? It paled next to the passion erupting inside her.

"So, here we are," Cassie continued. "You thinking I'd make a poor choice because I'd be sure to break your heart, and me, wondering what the hell I'm supposed to do with all these new and wonderful feelings."

Britt felt her breathing deepen. She set her glass next to Cassie's.

"Well, help me figure this out, Britt. Have any of your other lovers before this last one been straight?"

"No."

"So your relationships with them ended because things just didn't work out. Right?"

Britt nodded.

"Do you think that maybe your last relationship broke up not because your lover was straight, but because things just didn't work out?"

Britt paled. "Possibly." Cassie's simple logic was hammering her last mental barrier, a silly prejudice she had constructed to protect herself. Soon she would have nothing with which to shield herself.

"There are no guarantees in life, Britt. Our hindsight is great, but our foresight is pretty blurry. But by taking no chances at all, you're taking the biggest risk of all—missing out on your own life. You're wiser than that. I know you are."

They sat, face–to–face, eyes burning into each other. Britt felt the last of her defenses turn to dust.

"I want to be part of your life," Cassie said, her voice low and intense. "I want you to be part of mine. I'm willing to do my best to make it work. Are you?"

In response, Britt leaned forward. Their mouths came together in a long, slow kiss. Under the guidance of Cassie's hands, and without breaking the kiss, Britt joined her on the bed.

"Wow oh wow." Cassie sagged into Britt, who then lowered her to the spread.

Their mouths joined again, open and hungry. When they broke at last, Cassie brushed back strands of hair from the professor's eyes. "Lady, you had me worried there for a while." She rested her hand on Britt's shoulder. "Thanks for trusting me. I meant every word I said."

"I know." Britt gently slid Cassie's hand down to her breast. "That's why I'm here and not out the door." She saw Cassie's eyes attain a shine of intimacy and her lips part. Watching Cassie's growing arousal, Britt felt her own escalate. She eased Cassie's T-shirt out of her shorts, then unsnapped her bra and slid a hand around to the front.

Cassie stirred. "I love how you touch me. You're so gentle, so soft."

Britt tugged on the save-the-whales design on Cassie's cotton top. "Let's take Mr. Orca off," she said.

Cassie complied by raising her arms. Moments later, an assortment of clothing decorated the nearby chair like tinsel thrown haphazardly on a pine tree.

Lying against the pillows, the women clung to each other tightly. Soaking in the sensations of their passion, Britt gazed down at the spot where their breasts flattened together. She pressed herself into Cassie with abandon.

Cassie slid her hands across Britt's back as she accepted her lover's full weight. "My god," she said. "I thought I had a good imagination, but it wasn't even close."

Britt kissed her neck and shoulders, then trailed kisses down to her breasts. As she sucked and nipped and teased a nipple, Cassie arched her back. Britt stroked her thighs, slipped a hand between her legs and sought her wet heat. Cassie cried out, then began a rhythm of her own. Britt followed Cassie's lead in the sexual dance, responding to the whispered guidance, a "yes" here, a "harder" there. They rocked to a shared physical song until Cassie began to pant. She made a final thrust against Britt. Feeling her orgasm, Britt stilled. "I love you, Cass," she breathed, holding her tightly. She felt a tiny hug in response.

"Okay?" Britt asked after a long moment.

"Definitely." Cassie grinned. "This gal's in heaven."

"I never pictured heaven being this hot," Britt said, wiping dots of sweat from her forehead.

"Hot?" Cassie ran a finger along Britt's jaw line. "We're just getting warmed up."

As they laughed, their eyes caught again and they sought each other's mouth. As their kiss deepened, Britt felt a leg press into her. She began moving slowly, then increased the tempo.

"No, you don't," Cassie said playfully, rolling Britt over. "I get to touch you. Everywhere."

Britt opened for Cassie and thrilled to her touch. She moved against Cassie's hand, then felt her fingers enter her. She gasped in pleasure as Cassie dove into her depths, exploring her gently, then surfacing after a while to roam her folds of flesh. Britt sensed her muscles gathering force, like the sea responding to the tug of the moon. The power escalated into a solid splash of blue, rising higher and higher. Then she was there at the crest, with the water curling over and Cassie on top riding the tube, staying true as Britt's muscles exploded into convulsions. The climax dissipated into a silent calm, broken only by a litany of "I–love–you's" sounding somewhere above her.

"Whew!" Britt sighed.

Cassie showed her dimples. "It's the ultimate ride, huh?"

Britt turned on her side. "I've wanted you since the moment we met," she said as she touched Cassie's flushed cheeks.

"When you knocked me off my windsurfer?" Cassie teased.

"No, when you ran me down."

"No way."

Britt smothered the banter with another kiss and felt again the stir of desire. They made love again and again, spending their passion, then finding it renewed. At last they lay in each other's arms, exhausted, joyous, wondrously alive...and oblivious to the small green box, sitting on the desk at the foot of the bed, scratched with the initials of a murdered man.

Thursday morning in the Thera Museum, Britt moved sleepily. Try as she might to stay focused on her task, her mind kept slipping back to the previous thirty–six hours of lovemaking. They had stayed in bed all day yesterday—Cassie had called in a vacation day—and had finally managed about three hours of sleep last night. Even this morning after breakfast, they had made love before Cassie roared off to the Akrotiri excavation.

Now Britt labored in the back workroom, tidying up her research and rechecking a few of her references. Nothing, thankfully, that required careful thought or analysis. To her relief, the monkey ewer had not swung to another shelf since she had last seen it. It clung to its assigned spot.

Was this such a smart thing to do? Britt asked herself, getting involved with Cassie? But how could it not be? she answered. Everything feels so right with her.

But not here. Britt became aware of something amiss. Another ewer, this one with a series of blue dolphins swimming around the circumference, was not in its place, nor anywhere else.

"It's missing," Britt murmured. The second one in as many weeks. Or had it been mislaid as the previous one had? She could understand one error, but not two. If this one was missing for real, she'd tell Dr. Gavas. No more tiptoeing around. He and the museum director would have to correct the incompetence on the staff. Britt rubbed her bloodshot eyes. Then again, maybe she was so blasted exhausted that she couldn't find her own hand in front of her face, much less some pitcher.

Britt glanced at her watch. It was too late to worry—she and Cassie had a plane to catch. She'd have Jim track down the ewer next week when she returned from Athens. But, by god, she thought, if it was missing she wouldn't stay silent.

18

"From what we can tell, you've got some lightweights stomping around with oversized boots." Rich Marcello smoothed out the napkin under his Bloody Mary. A Sunday morning breeze swept across the tables lining the sidewalks of Kolonaki Square, full of the scent of cedars and edged by the pungent fumes of diesel engines. "The Alevras family is a one–generation dynasty, built from scratch by the father, Dimitris."

"How did he manage that?" Britt asked, signalling the waiter for another orange juice. The Americans sat in a far corner of an outdoor cafe in the quiet Athens neighborhood, away from the main cluster of clients.

"He was a flunky during the dictatorship back in the sixties and seventies. The higher–ups did time; he pleaded innocent and got off with six months in the slammer. Conveniently enough, he had a tidy pile of drachmas to buy land on Crete and take over a bumbling winery on Santorini."

"Some coincidence."

"Especially for some dirt poor islander. Puts on a uniform and the gold flows. I'd say the old man is as clean as a Sicilian mobster.

"Know how he got the money?"

"Nah. Who knows what happened back then. Chances are no paper trail ever existed. Not with a clever guy like Dimitris."

"But he came out of the dictatorship a wealthy man?"

"Filthy rich. Unfortunately, I wasn't able to get his bank records—or his son's."

The green canopy overhead flapped in the warm breeze. A stray tabby rubbed against Britt's leg, then moved on.

"Yeah," Marcello continued after taking another sip, "up-standing businessmen everyone claims. No dirty noses or bloody fingerprints. Interpol doesn't have a thing on them...yet. I keep thinking that Bountourakis stumbled on something."

"Finding his film box on Mesa Vouno clinches it for me."

"Circumstantial evidence, but what an eyepopper. There's got to be a link."

"I agree," said Britt. "So, do you have enough to send in a team of investigators?"

"Not yet. My contact in the C.I.S. says they won't haul Alevras in based on a Fuji box. The AK–47s those muscle men were carrying at the winery might be the trip wire, though. He's putting in the paperwork to open up an investigation now."

"It can't happen soon enough for me." Britt took a long sip of the freshly squeezed juice. "What should I do now?"

"Keep clear of the winery, Alevras, and his lackeys. But," Marcello said, stirring his drink with its celery stick, "keep your sights on them. There's a bit of the Three Stooges in these guys. They may stumble over each other again."

"What do you think they're up to?"

"Definitely not smuggling Minoan artifacts, even given your missing pots at the museum." Marcello crunched into the celery. "Too dinky for these guys. Probably drugs or arms."

"Hmmm..." Britt ran a thumb down the side of her sweating glass and wondered how she had become so fond of Marcello. His arrogance seemed more like confidence now, his overbearing manner merely energetic competence. Maybe being in love elevated the whole world. Whatever it was, Britt was glad he was on her side.

Marcello plunged the ragged end of the celery back into his drink. "So, Britt, what's got your eyes shining so bright these days?"

Britt felt a grin stretch to her molars. "I'm having a good time."

"Sounds like love. Who is she?"

"Cassie Burkhardt. How did you know?"

"The folks at the American School mentioned it, but I probably would have figured it out. My sister's gay. I've met some of her friends. It's sharpened my sensibilities."

"How did you get a security clearance with a lesbian sibling?"

Marcello laughed. "She was married when I applied for the job, thank god. The old boys in D.C. are still a bunch of provincial jackasses."

"I'm glad to hear you say that."

"Nothing they haven't heard from me directly."

The waiter stopped by the table, but Marcello waved him off. "So, does Cassie know what's going on?"

"She thinks Bounty may have been killed. I haven't told her about you or my little side project on Santorini."

"Good."

"For now, Rich. If I have to, I want to be able to tell her everything. I won't allow my work for you to threaten our relationship."

"I don't recommend your saying anything, Britt. But I'll let you be the judge."

"Thanks, Rich." Britt finished her juice. "What did you find out about the Kazantas family on Santorini?"

"Zippo. I think we can assume they're a harmless clan banking on a ticket to America."

"Anything else, Rich? Otherwise, I'll be off." Britt retrieved her handbag from under the table. "Got a busy day ahead of me. Cassie and I are going down the coast this

afternoon. We're seeing Nicki Lampas—Zerakis's god-
daughter—then on to Sounion."
"What's Lampas doing down that way?"
"Working on a housing project."
"Have fun. Stay in touch." Marcello jumped to his feet as
Britt stood up. "By the way," he said, "have you seen any-
thing of that guy who was following you around?"
"Not since the night I chased him down the alley."
Marcello sniggered. "I bet that's one experience he didn't
share with his buddies. Zerakis must have pulled him off once
you left for Santorini."
"Are you sure he's working for Zerakis?"
"Sure as I need to be. One of my assistants chatted him
up. The gold–plated M.P. denied everything, of course.
Threw a five–star tantrum, as a matter of fact. Said he'd never
interfere in the life of his godchildren by having their associ-
ates followed."
"You don't believe him?"
"Sure. And Elvis is conducting tours of the Acropolis."

Britt and Cassie took the scenic route south of Athens
along the jagged coastline. The road held a small number of
cars, most throttling to the beaches, with a few tour buses
bound for the tip of the peninsula. As they drove slowly to
enjoy the view, every vehicle but one passed Britt's rented
Saab 900 Turbo. The exception hung at a distance and
appeared not much more than a wavering heat mirage on the
horizon.
"What's this town we're going to?" Cassie asked, studying a Michelin map.
"Leurina. It's just north of Sounion."
"Found it," Cassie said, tapping the map in triumph. She
slipped the road guide into a pocket on the door, then reached
for Britt's hand.

"How are you doing?" Britt asked.

"Tired," Cassie said. "You're wearing me out. I'm loving every minute of it."

Britt kissed the middle knuckle on Cassie's hand. "Me, too."

"Do you think Anne and Bill mind us drooling all over each other at their apartment?"

"We're not doing that! We've been perfectly respectable."

"Apparently not. Anne's been looking at us a little sideways, don't you think?"

"The world's always at a thirty–degree tilt for her," Britt laughed.

"She is a dear. A mother hen, but a dear."

"Yep, she's one of my favorites. She approves of you, by the way."

"Does she?"

"Uh–huh. She thinks you're wonderful. Cute, too."

"Just wait. One more night without sleep and I'm going to turn into a mass murderer, minimum."

Britt grinned. "Remind me of that at three o'clock tomorrow morning, okay?" She slowed to take a left turn to Leurina. "Don't be surprised if Nicki invites herself along to Sounion. She can be rather forward. She'll probably want to check you out, too."

"Why don't we invite her and save her the trouble?"

"Would you mind?"

"No. I want to get to know your friends, especially if they're all like Anne and Bill."

"Well, she's certainly as lovable."

Cassie hesitated. "Were you two lovers?"

Britt shook her head. "A relationship with a student is a big no–no in my book."

"Glad to hear it."

"Nicki had one of those crushes that was both cute and annoying at the same time. Luckily we were able to maintain a friendship through it. She's a great kid, really. As loyal as they come."

Passing through the town square, Britt unfolded some directions she had jotted down. A few minutes later, they rolled up to a three–story building five blocks from the center of town. Nicki hurried to the curb to greet them, then escorted them around her masterpiece.

"Another miracle rising from blueprints into stucco," Nicki said at the conclusion of the tour. The three turned to admire the timbers of the eight–unit building wedged into a hillside. "On schedule and on budget."

"That's a miracle in itself," Cassie replied. "My company would give you a walnut plaque to hang in your office just for that."

Nicki grinned. "I have several of those already."

"What about the problems you mentioned?" Britt asked.

"Ah, the ones that brought me here for the weekend." Nicki repositioned her glasses and wiped a broad hand across her black hair. "The owners decide suddenly they want more closet space. I fixed it by moving some walls. Smaller utility rooms, bigger closets. Everyone is happy. Especially me— since the interior walls have not been put up yet."

"Easier to move walls on paper than in the building," Cassie said.

"Much," Nicki smiled. She turned to Britt, noting in her laughter a subtle resonance that she had not heard since their days at Berkeley. It was the sound of being in love. She knew instinctively that Britt and Cassie were sleeping together. It made her stomach burn for a moment.

"How did the symposium go last night? I'm sorry that I could not make it."

"A bore. No new ideas. Just venting of emotions—leave burial grounds alone or dig 'em up. Frankly, I'm sick to death of the subject."

"Did they say anything about the British Museum sending back all their plundered goods?"

"You bet. More than a few people got hot about it. But the moderator kept the focus on burial sites for the most part." Britt stepped around the litter of nails and scrap wood. "Well, we should push off, Nicki. The temple is waiting for us at Sounion. Want to come along?"

Nicki opened, then shut her mouth in surprise. "That's very kind. I would like that, yes."

"Good!" Cassie exclaimed, clapping her on the back. "Let's go."

"I'll bring my camera. You will have beautiful, official photos for your picture books."

"Great," Britt said. "Better bring a sweater in case we stay late."

Britt's car blazed along the two–lane highway south of Leurina. The cobalt Adriatic sea extended to the western horizon where it brightened under the collapsing light of the sun. Near shore, the water broke into rolling columns of white capped waves that moved in unison to the rugged shore.

As Cassie and Nicki talked about architectural software and computer–aided design programs, Britt withdrew into her own thoughts. She relished the temporary privacy. It seemed as if every moment for the past three days had been spent schmoozing with a colleague, making love with Cassie, or the two of them trying to figure out the next time they could.

She could hardly believe she was in a relationship again. But her return to the States loomed ahead. She and Cassie hadn't talked about what would happen once she left...even

if she did exchange her ticket for one giving her a couple of
extra weeks, the summer would end. What then?

Britt glanced into the rearview mirror. Nicki caught her
look. She held her eyes for one long moment, then winked.
She knew, and it was all right. Relieved, Britt slid her eyes
to the reflection of the road behind her. Again one car, tucked
safely in the distance, matched her speed. Box–like, hugging
low to the road, it appeared to be the same car that had
followed her earlier.

Pulling the Saab to the left around a blind curve, Britt
squeezed the brake pedal slowly to the floor.

"What's wrong?" Cassie asked.

"We're being followed," Britt said. "I'm sure it's the same
car that was behind us all the way from Athens."

Cassie and Nicki turned around in their seats.

"Don't look," Britt said. Both passengers assumed their
previous positions just as a green BMW came around the
curve. The driver, realizing that the Saab had slowed,
slammed on his brakes. Too late. By the time he had stopped,
Britt had a clear view of him in the rearview mirror.

"The guy with the dark beard," Britt said, speeding up.
"Well, we meet again."

19

"Who is it?" Cassie asked.

"Don't know. I've seen him before in Athens. Remember him from the Acropolis, Nicki?" Britt checked the mirror again. "Watch now. He should be passing in a couple of seconds."

As the 320i cruised by Britt, the driver turned his face away.

"Damn, I didn't get a good look," Cassie said.

Spotting a roadside cafe, Britt swung the Saab onto a patch of dirt that served as a parking area. A cloud of dust churned around the car, then rolled across the two small iron tables on the veranda. "How about you, Nicki?"

"No luck."

Britt studied the squat building, stuck in the middle of nowhere. "Either of you need anything while we're here?"

"Water," Nicki said quickly. She popped open the car door and disappeared into the dark interior of the restaurant.

"Come on, Britt, what's going on?" Cassie said as soon as Nicki was out of sight.

"I wish I knew," Britt replied. "This is the first I've seen him since I've come back to the mainland." She related the incident of chasing him down an alley.

"Did you talk to the cops?"

"I've let the authorities know," Britt said, smiling with reassurance. "Don't worry."

"Listen, if you're going to go after some guy in an alley, I'm worrying."

"He is gone?" Nicki asked, sliding back into the car. She handed a plastic bottle of spring water to the front.

"Probably not for good," Britt said, taking a long pull on the bottle.

Indeed, they didn't have long to wait. They spotted the BMW in the Sounion parking lot. Its driver was missing.

"Maybe we should tie him to a pillar until he tells us what he's up to," Cassie suggested. "The tourists would probably think it was part of a show."

"Great idea, Cass," Britt said, stopping the car at the entrance.

"Think he's got a gun?"

Nicki motioned for Britt to drive into the lot. "Go on. We're safe. No guns allowed in this country."

"Yeah," Cassie said dryly, "tell me about it."

"You know, we could shoot him," Britt said, easing her foot off the brake. "Right, Nicki?"

The Greek adjusted her glasses, then caught Britt's meaning. "My camera. Ah, yes. We will capture beauty today. And perhaps a bit of the ugly."

The trio hiked quickly up the hillside to the temple of Poseidon. Its white marble columns gleamed against the brilliant blue of the sea. Britt and Cassie stood at the southwestern tip of the ruins, peering inland, back at Nicki. Positioning herself halfway across the temple, the architect began snapping the first of several pictures.

From their vantage point, Britt and Cassie could see the stranger emerge from a row of foundation stones at the north side of the temple. With his hands cupped over his face, he lit a cigarette, then drifted toward the backside of the ruins.

As the women explored the site, Nicki took on the role of tour guide. "Notice these columns," she said, her bangs blowing back from her forehead. "They have only sixteen flutes instead of twenty. The fluting is more shallow than usual to give the column a slender look. Now," she continued, her voice dropping, "move to your left so I can take a picture of our friend."

Nicki shot Britt and Cassie framed against a row of huge marble columns where the pediment was still in place. Behind them, the blue sea sparkled, and in the far right border, the man appeared. "Wait!" Nicki cried, holding up her hand to the women. "Let me get a couple more." Quickly, she switched from the wide angle lens to a zoom. She perched on a column broken near its base and set a steep angle for the shot. Wild crocuses, wilted and dried in the cracks of the stones beneath her feet, jerked stiffly in the wind.

"He plays a poor tourist, doesn't he," Britt said to Cassie. She eyed the stranger, dressed in khaki pants and a white polo shirt, through her sunglasses. "He doesn't even pretend to enjoy the ruins, much less the view." By now, the man had made his way to the western edge of the structure.

Nicki focused her Nikon. A child's screech turned the stranger's head three-quarters of the way toward the Greek woman. She clicked the picture. The man's head jerked fully around to Nicki, his mouth twisting in anger.

Nicki swung the camera to the left and snapped another photo of Britt and Cassie, arm in arm, with big grins on their faces. But it wasn't quick enough. The man knew that his face had been recorded on film. He swore and scurried around the edge of the temple. He stopped one last time, in a cluster of tourists viewing Lord Byron's name scratched into a pillar, and glowered at the three who had outwitted him. Then he hurried to the exit and back to the parking lot. Moments later, he had his BMW screeching north.

"Why would someone follow me?" Britt echoed the question she had been asked. Her companions were enjoying beers at the open-air tourist pavilion adjacent to the ruins.

She watched the bottom of the sun drip slowly onto the
horizon. "I've been asking myself that question for three
weeks now. How may pictures did you get of him, Nicki?"
"Three, four not so good ones. One zoom of his face. That
should be all we need. I can blow it up big."
The table was small, the taverna quiet. Three couples sat
at different tables, each with red–and–white gingham cloths.
Two English couples enjoyed drinks only. A Swedish pair
ordered dinner from square menus written in English and
Greek.
"Could I have the film?" Britt asked.
Nicki started. "Why? I'll develop it when I go back to
Athens tomorrow. At the office."
"I'd like to see the pictures sooner."
"You can't get them developed faster. I will do it."
"Nicki, I have my own sources."
"I ask this of you. Let me help you. It is my honor to
develop this film. I bring it to you tomorrow morning, before
your plane leaves."
"Okay, I don't want to argue," Britt conceded, controlling
an impulse to snatch the camera from her and rip out the film.
An orange smudge on the horizon was all that was left of
the day. Britt felt the heat of the earth rise into the cooling
air. Above, the stars beat on the dark land. "Well, it's time to
head back to the city," she said, stretching out her fatigue.
"Let's hope that guy is long gone."

As they started up the coastal road, no BMW appeared.
Once past black pools of water used for salt drying, the road
straightened for a small stretch. It was then that headlights
flashed into view in the mirror. "I think our friend is back,"
Britt said. "He was parked on a side road waiting."
"He's probably pissed as hell at us for taking his picture,"
Cassie added.

"You're right," Britt said, failing to notice a second pair of headlights appearing behind the BMW. "Let's not mess with this guy any more." Her stomach shrank into a tight, cold sphere. She pushed the pedal to the floor. The Saab leaped into the night, its headlights stroking the roadside foliage as the car rushed by. Britt leaned back in the seat and let the steering wheel become part of her body. The Turbo sped around the curves of the snaking road, running for its life.

When the road straightened for a stretch, the pursuing car took advantage of it. It moved into the left lane and nosed alongside the Saab. Britt glanced over and saw the bumper, then the door. In an instant, the barrel of a shotgun appeared.

"Look out!" she cried, reaching for Cassie and shoving her down. A shot sailed over the car. Britt swerved to the right and onto the shoulder. She popped her head up and saw the car still adjacent to them. Her mind registered something else—a curve in the road, to the right. She pulled back onto the pavement. Another shot rang out. Britt slammed on the brakes. The companion car, its occupant fixated on the Saab, zoomed ahead and missed the curve. Airborne for a moment, the car and its red tail lights disappeared into the awful darkness, followed by a terrible crunch of snapping steel and breaking glass.

Britt angled the Turbo off on the shoulder and jammed on the parking brake. The car doors swung open and the three riders dashed across the road to the spot where the BMW had careened over the edge. Fifteen feet below them, it rested, smashed against a boulder twice its size. The driver's door had folded open. The man sprawled half in, half out of the car.

"His legs are pinned," Britt shouted as she led the charge through the sharp, dry brush.

As the three bent over the injured man, Nicki snapped on a miniature flashlight that she had pulled from her camera pack. "He's still alive. Barely."

Britt tugged on his legs, but couldn't budge him.

"Who are you?" Nicki asked in her native tongue. The man's eyelids fluttered, then closed to shut out blood streaming from a gash in his forehead. He worked his jaws, but no sound emerged. "Who sent you?" Nicki placed her ear directly over the man's mouth.

"Christ damn you," the man rasped in Greek.

"Tell me who you are. We will help."

"No." The man's eyes receded in fright.

"My son, my son," Nicki cooed into his ear, betting on his delirium. "Tell your mama. Tell your mama what you are doing following these pretty girls."

"Protect...protect..." The man's breathing was thin and jagged.

"Nicki," Britt said, putting a hand on her shoulder.

"He's dead anyway," Nicki said, turning back to the trapped man. "Tell me again."

The man's head slumped.

"Tell me you naughty boy!"

The man's jaws ground together painfully and a new surge of blood bubbled through his lips. Nicki leaned close for the breathy response.

"Hurt the American...hurt..." The man's head fell to the side. He coughed, then was still.

"What did he say?" Britt demanded.

Nicki closed his eyes. "Nothing but his prayers. His stupid prayers." She felt in the man's pockets. "No wallet," she said. "No identification." She rose slowly. "We should go."

Just then, they heard someone bounding down the embankment, crashing through the wild oleanders and scrub oaks. A middle–aged man yelled at them in Greek, waving his arms in the air. Nicki matched his tone, word for word.

"Shit," Cassie said, staring at the dead man at her feet. "Shit. I don't believe this. What a bloody mess."

"What's his problem?" Britt asked Nicki.

"He saw the accident. He wants to know what happened. I tell him the man is dead." While Mikos's godchild spoke to the women, the stranger made his way to the corpse and examined its features. He shook his head sadly at the three.

"Come on," Britt said, tugging Nicki's sleeve. "Let's call the police."

"Right. We go now." Nicki spoke again sharply to the newcomer, then searched for footholds in the hillside.

The Americans scrambled up after her. As they clamored to the shoulder of the road, the architect wheeled around. "Did any one check the glove compartment?"

Britt and Cassie shook their heads.

"Maybe his wallet is there. You wait here. I don't want that other guy to get it. I am back in two minutes."

At the wreckage, Nicki hailed the middle–aged man. "I thought you would not make it."

"I drive like a crazy man from Athens after your call to Mr. Zerakis. Your godfather thinks you are touched in the head."

Nicki shrugged. "I had no time to explain. My friends waited for me in the car while I bought water." The young Greek turned her attention back to the car and quickly ran her eyes over the twisted metal. She slipped an arm through the shattered window on the passenger side and flipped open the glove compartment. Maps and the owner's manual dropped out. "Damn," Nicki said. "Nothing here."

Using a Swiss Army knife, the man from Athens unscrewed the front and rear license plates and slipped them off the car. Kneeling next to the body, he deftly sliced off the fleshy portion of the dead man's left index finger, wound a handkerchief around it, then stuffed it in the pocket of his jacket. Then he picked up the victim's shotgun and hid it under his jacket.

"I am done here. I have everything I need." The man turned to Nicki, crouched by the car.

"Not quite," Nicki said, tossing him a roll of film. "Get that developed tonight." She loaded a new roll from her camera strap and quickly clicked to the end with the cap still secured over the lens.

"Done," the man nodded.

Halfway up the embankment, Nicki turned back in time to see the man flip a lighted match into a patch of dry vegetation a short distance from the car.

"Did you find anything," Britt asked Nicki upon her return.

"Nothing," she said. The man from Athens had now reached the road and half trotted to his car.

"We have to call the police," Britt said, turning to face Nicki.

"Let's go!" the Greek cried. "The first place we see we stop and call. But I give them no names."

Britt nodded. "No names."

"I'll stay in Leurina, though. I can find out more if I stay close."

"Good idea. What about the film? I want it developed."

Nicki struck her forehead. "Ah, the film. You take it." She began rewinding the film in her camera. "You get it developed in Athens. A good shop. Make copies for me, okay?"

"Okay," Britt said. She released the parking brake with a sigh of suppressed triumph. As she swung the Saab back onto the road past a small stand of cedars, a tremendous explosion from the wrecked car rocked the coastal highway.

20

"Nicki called the police from a phone booth, anonymously," Britt reported.

"You did the right thing." Rich Marcello's voice was calm and reassuring.

Britt gave Cassie a thumbs up. The computer programmer leaned against the kitchen counter, across from Britt who sat at a small table in the MacKenzie's apartment. Both Anne and Bill had gone to bed.

"Absolutely," Marcello continued. "Right now the last thing you want is the Greek authorities putting you under the light bulbs. No need for the uniforms to know about you. Nicki handled it like a pro."

"What happens if they do find out?"

"Your defense is airtight. He tried to run you off the road. He just killed himself instead of you."

"Aren't we lucky?"

"Do the MacKenzies know?"

"No. They were in bed by the time we got home."

"Keep them and everyone else out of it. Right now, it's just we four who know."

"Plus that guy who stopped after we did. And Mikos Zerakis. Nicki was going to call him from Leurina. Family duty."

"And family protection. It's a plus in a way. Zerakis will take care his godchild. He won't want her name splattered in the news about this. He'll put his sniffers on it—they'll be as discreet as British royalty used to be. I doubt I could pry anything out of him on this one. When do you two head back to Santorini?"

"Noon tomorrow. I'll drop off copies of the pictures from
Sounion at the embassy before we go."

"I'm counting on it. I'll run the guy's mug through Interpol. Listen. Be careful. Don't take chances. I'll call you in a
couple of days."

Britt hung up. "The embassy is handling it. Rich says not
to worry."

"Easy for him to say," Cassie scowled as she headed into
the bedroom. Britt followed. "He has diplomatic immunity.
We don't."

"You know, this isn't exactly the evening I had planned
for us," Britt said as she turned down the bed covers then sat
on the sheets.

"Really?" Cassie tossed her watch on the night stand
between the two single beds. "Today we get chased, shot at,
and see some bastard croak. I don't know what we could do
for an encore, except maybe chew through the bars of the
Athens jail with our teeth."

Britt shifted against the pillow upended against the headboard. "You're mad at me, aren't you?"

"I'm scared, but more than that," Cassie said, sinking next
to Britt on the mattress, "I'm hurt. You know more than
you're telling me. I don't like secrets. They're mean and
manipulative. For days, I've been marvelling at how equal
things are between us, and now, after today, I feel that I'm
left out of some big, important game that you're playing."

"Cass, it's not that I don't trust you."

"Bullshit, it's not. What's going on? What are you doing
with the home phone number of some guy in the Embassy?
Am I involved with Britt Evans or Jamie Bond? The first I
want, the second, you can keep."

As Britt examined Cassie's gray, flashing eyes, she knew
the time had come for disclosure. She took a breath and

plunged in. "I'm not a spy, Cass. But I think Paulos Boun-tourakis may have been."

"Bounty?" Cassie's face twisted with bitter amusement. "Never!"

"An informant, at least." Britt quickly recounted, under the promise of confidentiality, how she met Rich Marcello and wound up helping him on Santorini. "So, to answer your other question, I have Rich's number because he wanted me to call him if I found anything odd happening at Santorini. Because, like you, he thinks there may have been more to Bounty's death than we know."

"The guy who ran off the road—do you think he was part of it?"

Britt sighed. "I don't know. I'm too tired to think it through. Let's talk about it tomorrow. Okay?"

"Sure. Thanks for telling me," Cassie said, snuggling in close.

"Still mad?"

"No." Cassie's shoulders twitched as she fought a shiver. "I just flashed on that guy in the wreck. I've never seen anyone die."

"Me either. I've seen several animals die on the farm—never a human, though. It's eerie how the light drains from their eyes."

"Did this happen in a farm accident?" Cassie asked, touching the slight bump on Britt's nose.

"Nope. I played shortstop when I was an undergraduate. A ground ball took a nasty hop."

"Ouch."

"I made the play, though. A blazing, bloody throw to first."

"Good arm, huh?"

"Arms," Britt said, bringing them tightly around Cassie and drawing her down.

Mikos Zerakis looked out over his country, shimmering in the white light of a hot morning, and thought of darkness. Not the kind that brings relief to a steaming population at the end of a blistering day, but the kind that coaxes men to evil. There, to the south of him, past the tops of the palm trees dotting the National Gardens, past the vast stretch of apartment buildings and the still wider expanse of dry land and deep sea, men plotted ways to fill their pockets with more gold than a thousand people could spend in a lifetime.

"What do you think of, Mikos?" Nicki asked as she joined her godfather on the balcony.

"Of a war many years ago."

"The resistance?"

Zerakis dipped his head slightly. "I froze my toes, lost my teeth, starved, nearly died of disease. Why? Because the thought of a fascist rule—or the return of King George—was to me worse than death. So I fight and I lose. The monarchy returns. Democracy comes. The dictators come. Democracy returns. Sometimes I think we sit on a carnival ride spinning around and around."

Nicki leaned on the iron railing and sniffed the acrid air. "What do you see now as we spin?"

Zerakis clanged his gold worry beads, worn from years of anxiety. "I see a clown, Dimitris Alevras, a bastard from the dark days. He kissed the rump of the junta and, with his lips puckered, funneled millions of drachmas into his own pockets."

"Alevras. The name is not familiar."

Zerakis ushered his favorite goddaughter from the balcony of the government building into the brisk atmosphere of his air–conditioned office.

"The man at Sounion—he worked for Alevras. The photos you took, the print from the finger my aide brought back.

They confirm this. Yannis Thadion was his name. The pet of a dog."

Nicki picked up an eight–by–ten glossy from the glass coffee table near the balcony doors. The eyes of the stranger burned at her from the enlargement made from a photograph she had taken at Sounion.

"Santorini," the statesman said, thinking out loud. "A man falls off a cliff there, one who was a small–time informant for the C.I.S. A long–quiet lackey from the dictatorship who owns a winery there rumbles to life. Then an American agent appears in the form of a professor."

"Mikos, the last you have wrong. Britt Evans is a real professor."

"She cannot spy at the same time?"

Nicki rearranged herself on the white leather sofa. "No, not Britt."

"She has met with American intelligence. Richard Marcello from the U.S. Embassy."

"I don't believe it."

Zerakis lifted his heavy eyebrows at the young woman, then continued pacing. "I have my sources on the embassy staff. I know who comes and goes."

"Then she doesn't know what she's doing."

"Perhaps. The innocent make good eyes, sometimes. They see things with fresh sight. Now, the question is, what is there to see on Santorini?"

"You mention a winery?"

"It would make a good front, yes? You can have bills of lading, but who can say what is in the crates shipped in and out?" Zerakis clasped his hands behind his back and resumed his stride across the thick carpet. "On a lazy island like Santorini—the police only are for watching the girls and bandaging injured tourists for their return flight to Athens.

As long as Alevras's men are careful, they can do what they want."

Zerakis paced for a few moments in silence. "Are these Americans back on the island?"

"Yes. They left Athens today. I told Britt I would call her tomorrow with more information." Nicki chuckled. "She is as mad as a scorpion."

"What happened?" Zerakis asked, his eyes brightening.

"I switched the film on her. She expected to see pictures of the man who died, but instead she had only blanks."

Zerakis's rumbling laugh was edged with sadness.

"I told her the shop where she took the film made a mistake in developing it. I think she believed me."

The statesman picked up one of the photos of Britt and Cassie standing against the white pillars of Poseidon's temple. "American intelligence," Zerakis muttered, "has blundered into dangerous territory. It crushes the innocent—and not so innocent—beneath its gigantic feet." Among its victims would be two pretty American girls, he added silently to himself. It was a shame.

"Mikos," his goddaughter asked, "why not have Greek intelligence check into the matter? It can't hurt."

"Yes, it can. For the same reason this Richard Marcello and the C.I.S. send a girl to do his work. An intelligence agent would show like a mole on one's nose. There is no hiding strangers on a small island, eh? To send in agents would alert Alevras. He would tidy up the operation before we could catch him with evidence." Zerakis paused. "Then, my girl, if we are wrong about our suspicions, your godfather would look very silly. The Conservatives would make much of it in the next election."

Nicki stood up. "Then, I'm the one to send. I am a friend of Britt. To visit her is natural."

"It is a thing I would not ask of you," Zerakis shook his head sadly.

"You don't need to ask. I volunteer."

"No, child."

The intensity of Nicki's black eyes matched that of Zerakis. "Godfather, I must. I go with or without your blessing." He held her eyes and for once did not know what to say.

"I do it for love and honor, Mikos, for you and the professor, for I owe much to you both. Without you, I would not be where I am today. Without Britt, I would not know who I am."

"You will go, then," Zerakis said, acknowledging the fiery spirit before him. "Your father has told me you would make a good resistance fighter. I do not want you to fight. I want you to use your wits, as you did last night."

"Can you arrange passage for me on a ferry?"

"A ferry?"

"No metal detectors, Mikos. I will take weapons with me."

"Weapons? I can pull you out of legal trouble, but if you get in the way of bullets..."

"I won't."

"You know how to use a gun?" The statesman could not hide his shock.

"My brothers taught me. We went to the firing range many times in college. It is an American pastime."

"You have a gun now?"

"No. I need you to get one for me. Or two. I prefer Lugers. Also, give me plenty of ammunition."

"Great God! I cannot do such a thing!"

"You can and you will, Mikos." The young woman's voice resonated with power. "You will not send me in unprotected...and, yes, you will give me your blessing."

21

Tuesday morning the sun streamed through the high windows of the Thera Museum, flooding the basement work area. Britt's long fingers paddled the workbench. The ewer was still missing. After the terror on the road from Sounion, just how important was a thirty–four–hundred–year–old "pot," as Rich Marcello so eloquently called it? It was hard to get worked up about a piece of fired clay when death had come tapping at her soul.

Britt unpacked her notes and printouts from her briefcase and marvelled at how detached she had become from the objects of her study. A week ago, it took full discipline to concentrate on her research, when her mind bulged with fantasies of Cassie at the slightest lapse. Now, instead of being preoccupied with love making, she thought only of protecting Cassie. She felt something sinister lurking in the ashen hollows of Santorini. She'd never forgive herself if Cassie was hurt because of her.

Britt searched the cabinets and cubby holes halfheartedly for the ewer with the grinning dolphins, and she examined the checkout slips. But by ten o'clock, she decided the pitcher was not to be found and took a break.

When she returned from the employee lounge after a cup of coffee, discouraged but not totally defeated, she found Jim Larson making a hasty exit from the room. His green nylon backpack swung by one strap over his shoulder.

"Just the man I wanted to see!" she exclaimed, mustering up a mighty smile and grabbing his upper arm.

Jim blinked his eyes rapidly.

"Come in here a second, would you?"

Jim quick–stepped into the workroom, propelled by the professor's strength.

"I have something to show you," Britt said, releasing him. She ran her eyes along the cabinets lining the north wall. Like a magic rabbit, the ewer had appeared on the second shelf. Britt opened the glass door and carefully lifted the artifact out.

"Recognize it?" she asked, turning the picture of the sea mammals toward the young man.

Jim shrugged.

"You can do better than that, Jim."

"What do you want from me?" he said, angling his blue eyes at the floor.

"Why don't we start with the truth."

Jim shuffled his feet, his head bowed.

"You just returned this ewer to the cabinet, didn't you? Didn't you?"

"Don't be stupid."

"Listen. Ten minutes ago, this piece was missing. You come in and, eureka! Here it is, just where it should be. What am I supposed to think?"

"Why think anything?"

"Think about this—either you start talking now, or I get Dr. Gavas on the phone."

"Forget that shit!" Jim snatched the pitcher from Britt's hands and held it aloft like a football. "You want this?" He feigned a toss against the plaster wall.

"Put it down," Britt said, her voice low and calm.

"Then you shut up about this! Got it?"

"Smashing it isn't going to solve your problems. Help me understand what's going on, Jim."

Jim's arm dipped. "Damn you. I don't want your understanding."

"You'd rather have Gavas's?

Jim's face blanched to a new level of pale.

"Listen, I want to be on your side. Now what's going on?"

The programmer lowered his eyes to the floor.

"Come on. Tell me."

"Damn you," he said softly. He held the ewer out for Britt to take. She grasped the artifact with two hands and placed it on the work table.

"Sit down," she ordered.

Jim slumped on a stool and hung his head down. Britt dragged another seat next to his. She faced him squarely, her right elbow resting on the table.

"Are you stealing artifacts?"

Jim twisted his head from side to side.

"Borrowing them, then?"

"Yes," he said, his voice small and fragile.

"Why?"

His shoulders heaved. "Don't," he said. His large hands flew up to cover his cracking face. He tried to regain his composure, but failed.

Britt let him weep for a few minutes. She fetched a couple of tissues from a counter across the room and handed them to him. Jim blew his nose loudly; his eyes were wet and pink.

"What's going on?"

"He's making me do it."

"Jim..." Britt's patience had become as fragile as the ewer.

"Irene's father." Jim pulled his white shirt out of his pants and wiped his eyes on the tails. "After Irene and I first started going out, he asked if he could see a vase, any vase with a pattern that hadn't been put on public display."

"To see it?"

"He wanted to make duplicates so when the original went on exhibit at the museum, he'd have copies already made for sale. He'd be ahead of the other merchants by months. So I did it, to impress him, and to impress Irene."

"Why? You have enough value on your own. You don't have to buy anyone's affection. Certainly not Irene's. She loves you as you are. I'm sure of it."

"It's hard to know sometimes. I want her to be happy. Pleasing her damn old man always cheers her up. I don't know, Britt. I want her in my life so much. Sometimes I get scared that she's going away—that her father will take her away."

"So, what happened?" Britt asked softly.

"I sneaked a vase out. In my daypack, for godsake. That's how easy it was. A few days later, after he was finished with it, I brought it back. No one noticed. It was simple. Until you came." Jim blew his nose again. "I knew you'd be looking things up, so whenever I took an artifact, I temporarily removed all references to it on the data base. I stored it in a hold file. Then, when the artifact was back in place, I'd reinsert the data into the main storage files."

"You missed a reference on this last one."

Jim's eyelids snapped shut like traps. "I'm not surprised," he said, opening them wide. "Gavas was buzzing around like a manic bee that night. I got nervous and careless."

Britt pursed her lips. "So, you just kept borrowing the artifacts?"

"Listen, I hated it. After the first time, when he wanted me to do it again, I refused. The bastard said he'd go to Gavas and the cops. He'd tell them I had stolen some artifacts and tried to sell them to him, but being the good citizen that he is, he had made me return them to the museum. The goddamn ass. I should have smashed him right then."

"But you believed him."

"Obviously. I didn't see any options." Jim shook his head, trying to throw off the nightmare. "But the worst part...the worst part..."

Jim reached for another tissue.

"The worst part was that I told Kazantas that you had noticed the ewer missing—the one with the monkey motif."

Britt nodded encouragement.

"I thought that would scare him into stopping. It didn't. Then when I heard...when I heard that one of his sons—Georgios—had almost hit you with that crate at Athinios, I knew that hadn't been an accident."

"Jim, he wouldn't hurt me for that!"

"Wake up, Madame Professor. We're talking about the family's lifetime pass to America. To a desperate kid, that's enough. He said he did it on impulse—the first time—if that's any consolation, but only to hurt you."

"The first time?"

"That hydrofoil incident was the second. He stole it and tried to run you over. He was royally skunked. He'd matched me ouzo for ouzo at a taverna. We were talking about things—he told me then about how he aimed that crate for your head. He said he needed to get the job done right. He ran off. I didn't know what idea was knocking around in his skull. I wasn't in much shape to care, either." Jim pinched his eyes shut, then sighed. "I'm the ticket, I'm the pipeline to the big time for that family. They still think that Fort Knox paves the alleys of America. You threatened that if you blabbed to Gavas."

"I'm a threat for real now. To him, to his family, and to you, Jim."

"I'd never hurt you. Georgios promised me he'd never do anything crazy again."

"Yet you continue with this shell game?" Britt picked up the ewer sitting in front of them and examined it. "Are you sure he's giving you back the real thing?"

Jim nodded. "I still have a few working brain cells. The first vase I gave him, I put a small chalk mark on the inside.

He'd have to use a flashlight to see it. He gave me back the same vase, I'm sure of it."

Britt frowned. A good art forger would have duplicated the thin white slash. She quickly studied the ewer. The design was clean, the lines incised with precision. If pressed to give an opinion, she'd say she held the original, not an imitation.

She turned back to Jim. "How many times have you done this?"

"Six."

"This is a real mess, you know."

"What are you going to do?" he asked, turning his bloodshot eyes on Britt.

She set the ewer back on the table. She scanned his puffy face. "This is the last time it happens?"

"I promise." Jim drew his palms over his mottled cheeks, rubbing away the tears.

"What are you going to tell Irene's father?"

Jim frowned. "That I was caught and I promised never to do it again."

Britt slid off the stool. "I'm not going to do anything right now, Jim. It seems that the only casualty in this whole matter has been your integrity. And perhaps the pocketbooks of a few merchants. It's been a foolish episode on everyone's part."

"I agree. I was the biggest fool of them all." Jim crossed the room to throw his tissue away.

Britt turned to him suddenly. "Do you think anyone suspected anything before this?"

"I don't think so. Why?"

"Could Paulos Bountourakis have discovered an artifact missing and believed it had been stolen?"

"I don't think so. He didn't spend much time here in the museum."

"How about the day he died. Did you see him around here then? Did he act funny?"

"He was bumming around the excavation. It was a Sunday. He seemed his normal self. Nothing unusual."

"You didn't see him that evening?"

Jim shook his head. "No. I was here in Thera. I had dinner with Irene's family, then hung around the store. I didn't see anyone from the excavation that night. The only person I saw was Bob. He trotted past the store about eight o'clock."

"Bob Collins? I thought he took a plane back to Athens late in the afternoon."

Jim shrugged. "It was Bob. I'm sure of it."

"Just checking in," Britt said.

"Where are you calling from?" Rich Marcello asked, his voice warm.

"The phone company in Thera."

"No news about the accident victim. The police say all the identification was stripped from the car. The cops are checking dental records, but that could take weeks. Anything down your way?"

"A question."

"Aim and fire."

"When you checked the background of the people at the Akrotiri excavation, did you check out a Robert Collins?"

"That's a negative, I believe. Let me check the file." After a few moments of silence, he came back on the line. "No. Who is he?"

"He's a friend of Cassie Burkhardt. He's spent quite a bit of time down here. Mostly on the weekends. He's a student at the American School. He graduated from the University of Pennsylvania, I believe."

"Do you want me to run a check?"

"If you could."

"What's your concern?"

"I don't know. A few things just don't fit together."

"All right, I'll do it. I should have a report this evening. Should I call?"

"I'd appreciate it. I'll be at the number I gave you before."

"Got it. Anything else?"

Britt paused. "I don't like what I've gotten myself into, Rich. I don't want people to get hurt."

"Britt, somebody put you on the playing field. You didn't and I didn't. Remember, you were tailed before we ever met. You had no choice in the matter. The one plus is that you have me in your corner."

"Then you'd better be ready if I need you."

22

"You should be on Santorini minding the winery," Dimitris Alevras said, picking up a crystal carafe of water off the bar and pouring a splash into a glass of ouzo. "Go home."

"Someone must speak sense to you," Sophia Delopsos said, wagging her finger. "Your son is out of hand."

"Theo is a poor imitation of a son." The elder Alevras examined the billowing liquid clouds forming in the liquor as though studying tea leaves. Fortification in hand, he turned to face the cold, pinched face of his sister–in–law. She stood halfway across the expansive living room, wrapped in a traditional black dress, hands on her broad hips.

"Then it is you who have made him so, comparing him every moment of his life to you. You do not make children from cookie cutters of their fathers."

"You need to tell me this!" Alevras cried, running his palm over the top of his head. His oiled hair held firm, like a flat slab of salt and pepper granite. "He is a lazy fool who squanders a father's fortune!"

"Your fortune...your fortune. It is the devil's money."

"It has given me pleasure." Alevras strolled to the bank of floor–to–ceiling windows on the north side of the room and observed a slice of his holdings. A gardener labored at a bed of azaleas by a small grove of cedars. Down by the beach, one of his men painted the bottom of a fishing boat while gulls wheeled overhead. To the west, a ship edged south toward the harbor of Heraklion, Crete.

"You would have me give this up?" Alevras flashed a row of straight, yellow teeth. The mustache on his broad, coarse face twitched at the unfamiliar expression.

"I suggest only that you be satisfied with what you have. You do not need more."

"How is it that you know what I need?"

"I know God. If you did, you would know, too."

"I know what it is like to eat dirt, I have been so poor. I know what it is a lose a wife."

Mrs. Delopsos held back a snort. He paid no attention to his wife when she was alive. He slept with harlots and took joy in telling her of it. Many times her sister had come running to her, her eyes streaming, her heart broken in a hundred pieces.

"I have lost a son, also," Alevras sighed, tapping the top of his glass with a short, fat finger. "Theo is not fit to be called mine. After this business, I cut him loose."

A shrill laugh exploded from Sophia Delopsos. "That I should like to see. He will put a knife to your throat."

"He hasn't the balls." The father grimaced at his dashed expectations. His son was to have been his partner, the seed that grows into the plant to replace the older generation. "From the seed of an oak has sprung a shaft of wheat." He moved to the U–shaped sectional in front of the windows. A table of white marble speckled with pink stood in the middle of the arrangement.

"In some ways, life has been cruel to you, Dimitris, but that is no reason for you to be so."

"You should speak," he said, extracting a Turkish ciga-rette from a silver box on a side table. "What do you have to tell me about Theo that I already do not know?"

"That in some ways, he is his father's son." Mrs. Delopsos crossed her skinny arms. "He uses the winery for nasty business."

"Eh?" Alevras held the thin cigarette midair and fastened his dark eyes on his sister–in–law.

"The crates of grapes we receive from here—that is a joke in itself—they contain more than grapes. We export more than wine."

"You are a foolish woman," Alevras said, striking a match and holding it to the tip of the dark tobacco roll. After the cigarette held its light, he silently blew out the match's flame.

Mrs. Delopsos tightened the fold of her arms. A self–satisfied smile twisted across her face. "You forget who runs the company. Your son does in name only."

"You forget whose money and whose men revived the winery." Alevras flicked the match into an ashtray. "I will do anything I please with the business. I do not need your approval."

"So, you are behind it. You have put Theo up to it."

"Theo lacks the brains," Alevras held a finger to his temple, "and the ambition," then thumped his chest, "to deal in the business. I bring deals to him on a platter, and he would rather sail his yacht with a thousand women than help his father. But he obeys my orders this time. He knows great riches are in store for him."

"What is it that you are planning?"

"I plan nothing. I help those who have dreams to realize them. I sell them what they need. What is wrong with that?"

"If the dreams are those of madmen, then your soul is forfeit."

Alevras eyed Mrs. Delopsos, picking out as he did so the hairline of his wife and the curve of her nose, in the sagging face of Sophia. Would his wife have aged so badly had she lived? God forbid. "What is it that you want?"

"Take Theo and his friends from Santorini. I want to run a decent winery, one that your sister would have been proud of. One that does not shame me. My friends talk to each other of these hooligans."

Alevras shrugged. It was a small thing she asked, really. He could do without the winery. He had a dozen other fronts he could channel his business through. And, after the coming shipment, he would have to install one of his own men at the winery because Theo would no longer be around. "Let me think on it and pray to the soul of my dear wife for guidance."

The phone whirred. Alevras punched a button on the black console on a corner table. It was from the *Praxis*.

"We have a very fine product, Mr. Alevras. Full bodied and sweet."

"Good. When do I taste this marvel?"

"Very soon. We cork the last bottles this afternoon. We should have a few cases delivered early tomorrow morning."

"Excellent. Will you accompany the shipment?"

"Yes."

"Theo, also?"

"He will. He'll accompany the cargo with me."

"Then the job will be done, eh?"

"Exactly as you wish."

After the connection had broken, Theo slammed his receiver into the cradle of the phone. Was his father pleased with nothing he did? The old bastard did not think that his son had the brains to monitor calls from the yacht. His father was the fool, not he.

What was this bullshit about his accompanying the cargo? Why should he fly to Cyprus with the shipment? Whose plan was that? Not his. What was his father up to?

The young Alevras pressed his face against the porthole of his cabin. The *Praxis* sliced through the rolling sea toward the Therian harbor. Damn them all, he thought. I don't need you. He padded up to the pilot house to check the course and ETA. Arrival time remained firm at sixteen hundred hours.

The strong afternoon winds pulled at the canvas awning that framed the small enclosure. Wishing to escape the buzz of electronic equipment and the sullen first officer, Theo stepped outside. The static of gadgetry was replaced by the low whistle of wind, the thump of the yacht as she cut through the waves, and the clang somewhere of metal against metal.

He had not made much of his life, the young Alevras thought as he leaned against the railing. That he would grant any stranger except his father. He had done poorly in school: why study when he would never need to work? He had loved poorly: why have one woman when money can buy many, at least for a few hours? He spent his life skipping from one pleasure to another. That, and doing his father's bidding. Why? He had his inheritance to think about. He didn't have to do the bidding with enthusiasm, though. It was his source of control and pride. The more his father worked, the more he lounged. The more fanatical his father became, the more indifferent he pretended to be. He couldn't be totally unconcerned, however. He would use his father for money, just as his father used him in all his money–making schemes.

He was to go with the shipment? Theo turned the idea over and over in his head. It did not make sense. He had not agreed to such a plan. It had never been discussed. Suddenly, he shivered. Did they intend to put him in one of the crates? Alevras grabbed onto the railing with both hands to steady himself. Could it be? Would his father do such a thing? He knew the answer. His imagination reeling, the Greek staggered below to his quarters.

23

Three short blasts of the ferry's deep horn propelled Nicki upright on the narrow bunk. She blinked at the small cabin, with its forty–watt bulb above a miniature dresser. Where was she? Milos, maybe. Was that a port of call on this route? The power of the mammoth engines reverberated through the steel hull. The ferry rocked to port, then to starboard. The passage continued.

Edging herself off the thin mattress, Nicki fixed a drink from a supply of Metaxis in her bag. How in God's name did I get myself into this? she wondered. She hated water, and here she was being tossed like a sack of onions in this tub. Worse, she hated the anticipation, and being alone with it. But aloneness was a suit that had come to fit her well.

As she screwed the cap on her flask of brandy, she heard a faint clink of metal. The doorknob to the room turned slowly. Knowing that the feeble lock would not hold against even modest pressure, Nicki sprang across the room and rammed her shoulder against the door. She clawed at the door knob, trying to stop the intruder from turning it. But the weak lock gave way, and a sliver of hallway light appeared.

Before Nicki could cry out, two men burst into the room. One of them pushed the young Greek back on the bed. A metal bar across the bottom of the frame snapped at the shock and clanged on the linoleum.

"We have some business to do, Lampas," Anton Vrouvas spat out. A sneer spread across his wide, oily face. He was a huge, square man who barely fit through the doorway. His frayed brown suit smelled of fish oil.

His partner, better looking and leaner by half, closed the door quietly. Dios Genoulis, dark like his companion, wore a green shirt and black trousers. "Make a sound and we hurt you bad."

Nicki eyed her duffel bag. It contained two Lugers and six clips of ammo. How she had fought for them, and now they were out of reach!

"We like to hurt you," the smaller guy said. "Maybe cut off two, three fingers. Your drawings would look funny then. Think so, Anton, they would look funny?"

"Maybe she could design holes in the ground."

"Graves, eh?"

"What do you want?" Nicki asked, keeping her voice even.

"You see your two girlfriends in Santorini?"

"I make no plans."

Vrouvas whacked her across the mouth with a palm the size of a horse's hoof. "You lie." He extracted green plastic worry beads from a jacket pocket and began to work them through his thick fingers.

Nicki licked blood from the corner of her mouth and righted her glasses. "I'm not lying. It's a surprise visit."

"Our friends will surprise them before you do. They will have some good times with them. Maybe Anton and me can join in." He winked at his partner.

Nicki tried to struggle to her feet, but the large man pushed her back on the bed.

"You worry? That's good." Vrouvas picked up the duffel bag. "Heavy," he said, shaking it like a martini. He dropped it on the floor and the metal inside clanked.

"What do you want?"

"You do not look so innocent. Our Yannis dies because of you. One of Zerakis's boys delivers this bag to you at the dock at Pireaus." Vrouvas toed the canvas sack with a scuffed leather shoe. "So, you go to do what? Kill Theo? Take the winery? Stop the airplane? You watch too many American movies. You become as stupid as these Americans. You are alone. We have many people."

Perspiration spread across Nicki's back. She shut her eyes, trying to think of her options.

"We are not barbarians, Lampas. Our boss tried the easy way with you and the American—run you off the road, put you in the hospital for a while, keep you away from Santorini until our work finishes, yes? But, you do not cooperate, so we do not cooperate. Understand?" Vrouvas turned his round, grizzled face to his partner. "Do you think this one understands?"

"You, Lampas, you are nothing," Genoulis snarled. "I prefer to cut off your fingers and make you eat them."

"Then why don't you?"

He stepped toward Nicki, but Vrouvas grabbed his arm. "No," the big guy said to his partner. "You," he commanded the young woman, "you sit. No talking."

Nicki complied, but her mind churned like a jet engine as she made her plans for the next port of call: Santorini. It would be her one and only chance.

"Nothing like Greek water!" Britt exclaimed swallowing half a glass. "Best in the world. Want some?"

"I had my fill out there," Cassie said, waving at the sea. "I think about half a dozen waves swan–dived right into my stomach on that last run."

A handful of sunbathers ambled up from Kamari Beach as the mid–afternoon sun weakened enough to justify abandoning their plots. A pelican sat contentedly on a post, while a sleepy, yellow dog eyed the bird, but hadn't the energy to chase it off.

Andreas glided toward the table on the veranda, pen and order pad in hand. "Something for you, Cassie?"

"I'm famished. How about sharing some stuffed grape leaves, Britt? Maybe some bread?"

"What about dinner?"

"Can't wait."

Andreas scratched down the order, then sauntered toward the kitchen.

"So tell me more about Bob," Britt said.

"Jealous?" Cassie grinned, tousling her wet hair in the hopes that the breezes would dry it quickly.

"Never. He just seems a curious fellow."

"He plays at being a student."

"What's he really about?"

Andreas placed a basket of pita bread and a bowl of cucumber dip on the table.

"He's a dig bum."

"Yes. He mentioned something about dropping in at excavations. Did you ever go with him?"

"Nuh–uh. A couple of times I wanted to—especially the time he went to Rhodes. He wanted to be off on his own, though. I didn't press him."

"How did he decide where he wanted to go?"

"I don't know." Cassie tore off a corner of the half moon of bread and dunked it in the yogurt sauce. "He'd just up and say, 'I'm going to Cyprus on Wednesday,' or more likely, 'Gee, I'm sorry you couldn't reach me. I was digging at Rhodes.' Real swell guy."

"How did he manage to dig at these sites? A person just can't stroll onto the grounds and roll up his sleeves."

"Don't ask me. Ask him." She folded the bread into her mouth. "What's this about anyway?"

"It's about his not going back to Athens as early as he said on the Sunday Bounty died."

Cassie face froze. "What do you mean?"

"Jim saw him that night in Thera."

Cassie swallowed hard. "That's impossible. I dropped him off at the airport."

"But you didn't watch him board?"

"No. I never did. He always wanted to be at the airport an hour and a half before departure. What a yawn."

"Do you think he could have gone back into town?"

"Maybe. But why?"

"That," Britt said, thoughtfully tearing off a chunk of bread, "is the question."

Genoulis tossed his hunting knife toward the ceiling. The carved handle twirled twice before the Greek snatched it on its way down. Vrouvas, meanwhile, claimed the bed opposite Nicki. With his legs spread and feet flat on the floor, he gawked at the petite woman who had twice his IQ.

The engines had been slowing for some time before Nicki realized it. When she became aware of the drag, she waited alertly. Her time neared. At the sound of the horn, Nicki bolted for the door. But with one swing of his giant paw, Vrouvas knocked Nicki back on the bed. His partner's knife clattered to the floor.

"You make me miss. For that alone I will kill you," Genoulis muttered to the architect sprawled across the bed as he retrieved his weapon.

Her face to the wall, Nicki feigned unconsciousness. She had been prepared for the blow and had managed to blunt its impact. As she tried to regulate her breathing, she heard passengers shuffle along the corridor outside her cabin. The sounds of life called out to her: babies crying, children chattering, women talking loudly of the bakery goods they would buy for dinner.

The smaller man leaned over Nicki, watching the steady rise and fall of her breathing. "You hit her too hard, you ox," he said.

"Bah!" Vrouvas replied, extracting a toothpick from his pocket. "She will live. Maybe it improves her sight."

Genoulis secured his knife in his belt. "We wait until the other passengers are off the ship. Then we help our seasick friend off. The *Praxis* will be waiting in the harbor."

"If we can rely on Theo." Vrouvas snorted. "We must get this one aboard quickly. No fuss." He slapped his partner on the shoulder and drew up a chair to talk quietly of the evening's plans with his partner.

After the noise of the departing passengers had abated, Vrouvas grabbed Nicki by the arm and pulled her to her feet. "Let's go!" he cried. His partner held open the cabin door.

Once in the passageway, the men each looped an elbow through Nicki's unresisting arms. Nicki staggered more than walked and kept her head lowered on her chest. Her one chance, she thought as they maneuvered her along the corridor, was to make a break when they went down the steps to the lower decks. The narrow stairways would allow only the width of one person.

At the first stairwell, Nicki made no move. Groggily, she followed Vrouvas, who went first, with the smaller man bringing up the rear. When they reached the third level and began descending to the deck used for debarkation, Nicki again hung onto the railings as she took one unsure step after another. Midway down, before Vrouvas had reached the bottom, she knew the moment had come.

In a burst of motion, Nicki swung herself over the railing and landed in a crouch on the deck. She sprang forward and ran along the deck, pushing aside the passengers straggling toward the gangplank. Behind her, she heard Vrouvas yell, and she knew he would be in full pursuit. Carrying the duffel bag filled with weapons, Genoulis would be slower.

Nicki flew off the gangplank and ran at full speed to the cable cars, north of the steps that zigzagged up the face of the cliff. Passengers from the ferry filled the loading area as they waited for the lift up to the city of Thera.

"Excuse, please. Excuse, please. Sorry." She pushed her way to the front of the line, through grumbling tourists, and slipped into the last of the six small compartments just before the door closed.

As the cable car jerked upward and began its ascent, its cables rolling over large, black wheels, Nicki spotted her tormentors waving their arms at the operator. She leaned back in relief, then realized they were looking past the cars, signaling someone at the top of the cliff. She wrenched her neck around and spotted two bruisers as big as the ones she had left behind. They would be ready for her at the top of the cliffs.

When the door of her cable car snapped open, Nicki took two steps across the platform, then bolted to the left. She leapt on top of a whitewashed retaining wall. Two more leaps and she gained a walkway of the town of Thera.

It was a bottleneck, though, the only path into the town proper. Below her, the men who wanted her; above her, next to her, the wall of the cliff. She raced along the stony walk, past an open area where the fat, squat palm trees of the old museum sat like corpulent kings. She had only twenty meters on them. They broke through gaggles of tourists like a bowling ball through pins, and burst onto the main pathway, their prey in sight.

"Damn those desk humpers in Washington. Can't they dig up the background on one American student in something under a century?"

Alexander Stamos cradled a scotch and let his friend Rich Marcello spout. "As I said, Interpol has nothing."

"Yeah. One hour after I put in my query." Marcello gazed without appreciation at the subdued blues of an evening sky outside his office window. "What the hell's the problem Stateside?"

"That is a question we Greeks ask often."

An aide opened the door and handed him a folder. "Your report. Just in over the fax." he said, then withdrew.

"About time." Marcello flipped the file open as he made his way to the desk. In the motion of seating himself, he suddenly plopped into his chair.

"What?" Stamos asked.

"Did I know this, or what? It couldn't have been simple." Marcello's eyes travelled down another page. "Robert Collins died nine years ago in a car accident. In the States."

"Then who..."

Marcello held up his hand like a traffic cop and skimmed down the page. Without looking at the Greek investigator, he punched the buttons on his phone. "I've got to reach Britt," he explained. "Warn her."

Stamos lit a cigarette with the one still burning. His mind was already racing with half a dozen scenarios.

A quizzical expression crossed Marcello's face, then he holstered the receiver. "Goddamnit! Phone service to Santorini has been cut off," he said. He punched another button on his console. "Donna, book me a seat on the next flight to Santorini. Have a rental car waiting—if there's any way they can reserve one at this end."

"Make that two seats," Stamos said, already gathering up his papers.

"Make it two seats," Marcello barked into the receiver. "After you do that, Donna, track down Mikos Zerakis. I don't care if you have to haul him off the floor of Parliament or out of his mistress's bed. I want him. Now."

24

"Damn it, find her!" The man who called himself Robert Collins hammered on an oblong table in a back room of the Santorini airport. His face was flushed an angry red.

"We try." Theo Alevras held a walkie–talkie in place with his jaw while he straightened a picture of the Greek flag that had slid askew.

"Goddamn bunch of idiots, all of you!"

"Quiet, please." Alevras listened intently for a few moments, then jammed the antenna into the receiver and set it on the table. "My men search still in Thera for Nicki Lampas. Perhaps we find her, perhaps not. She cannot telephone for help. Anton blew up the phone company. Poof! It is gone. When we find Lampas, she will be with the Americans."

The air was close in the small, crowded room. Five fully armed guards, some in jeans, others in makeshift fatigues, sat as still as the worn tables and chairs. The room reeked of sweat and smoke from Turkish cigarettes. Outside an Olympia Airlines prop plane set down under the sharp lights of the runway. It was the last scheduled flight of the night.

"So how do we know Britt doesn't have a radio transmitter in her room? She could call off the island."

Alevras held his hands out in a supplicant's pose facing the table, and rolled his eyes toward heaven. "He goes mad now, yes?" Connecting again with his partner, he continued. "She has nothing in her room. This I have checked. The maid at her pension is on my payroll."

Collins snorted.

"The last plane is on time. After it leaves, we shut down the airport and have it to ourselves, like other times."

"Dream on. What about the time we caught Bountourakis snapping pictures of the airstrip from that goddamn mountain, just like this was some movie set? No screw–ups, no witnesses this time. I'm going to make sure of that," Collins said, checking the ammunition in his Beretta 92F.

"What will you do?" The Greek eyed the American suspiciously.

"Say good–night to a couple of American chicks. Maybe even find me Mikos Zerakis's little friend."

"This gun—do you need it?"

"I call it the problem solver," Collins said, zipping on a navy windbreaker over the 9–mm weapon. He gave the nylon shoulder holster a final tug, then disappeared out the door.

The sun had dipped behind the curtain of mountains southwest of Cassie's pension, turning the ashen fields of the surrounding area to a charcoal gray. Inside, Britt and Cassie lay quietly, drifting from dream to dream, stirring occasionally to physical need, only to be recaptured by the weight of exhaustion. Doors slammed down the hallway as vacationers hurried off to dine along the beach front. Crickets scraped out their mating tunes in the choking dust by the patio.

Someone tapped softly, then more loudly, on the door.

"I don't want to answer," Cassie said, tightening an arm around Britt.

"Could be important. I'll get it."

"No, stay here."

But Britt, already halfway out of the bed, had a white caftan in her grasp. She dropped the cotton robe over her shoulders as she made her way to the door.

"Well, get rid of them pronto," Cassie ordered.

Britt slid back the bolt and opened the door. Nicki stared at her from the hallway, her eyes wide and wild.

"What happened!" Britt cried, drawing her friend into the room.

Nicki toppled forward. Taking her arm, Britt steered her into the desk chair.

"What's going on?" Cassie scooted up to the headboard, drawing the sheet up to her chin.

Nicki's eyes roamed around the room; she didn't seem to understand or care about the scene she had entered. "We are in trouble. Much trouble."

Britt tossed Cassie a robe. The programmer maneuvered into it under cover of the cotton sheet.

"Center yourself, Nicki," Britt said softly. She fetched a bottle of Metaxis from under the night table and dumped a couple of shots into a water glass.

"We must be quiet. Okay?" Nicki tossed back a large hit of the brandy.

"We won't scream," Britt smiled, her voice soothing. "Promise. Now, tell us what's going on." She propped herself on the bed's baseboard and bent forward, elbows on her knees.

"It's a long story, but I keep it short. Theo Alevras and his father are smuggling something to Cyprus tonight. What, I don't know." The young Greek fortified herself with another slug of the potent liquor. The pain of her wounds lessened as the brandy warmed her belly. "They smuggle it in crates from the Fira Winery."

"Are you sure?"

"This I know. For sure." Nicki slipped off her glasses and cleaned the lenses with her shirt tail as she told her friends about what she had learned from Mikos and from her experiences aboard the ferry. "Now, listen to me," she said, looking at the Americans with wide, naked eyes. "These men, they planned to kill me. They say others would take care of you."

Cassie slipped into the bathroom and returned with a wet cloth. "Who else knows what's happening at the winery?" she asked, handing Nicki the folded square.

"Besides those involved, the three of us." She ran the terry cloth over her face, then wiped a sweaty neck. "I try to call Mikos, but the lines are dead. No phone service anywhere on the island, no inter–island, no connection to anything."

"Is there a flight going out anytime soon, Cass?"

Cassie retrieved her Seiko from the nightstand. "No. The last one took off fifteen minutes ago."

"You listen to me," Nicki said. "I go to the Athinios dock. Maybe a ship can radio Athens with ship–to–shore."

"We'll drive you there, Nicki. Or I will, if you don't want to go, Cass."

"No, we go together."

"Right." Britt's mind raced. "While you dress, I'll run back to my place. I want to see if I got a message from Rich Marcello before the phones went out."

"Marcello, from your embassy?" Nicki asked.

"Yes. How did you..."

"Mikos has his sources."

"Better put on some warm clothes while you're there," Cassie advised.

Nicki set her finger on the face of her watch. 10:15. "Can you do this in ten minutes? No more?"

"Less than that. Cass, you can be ready by then?"

"Changed and waiting."

Britt left through the French doors and dashed down rows of pistachio trees to her pension.

Cassie took in the tattered young woman in front of her. "You've been very brave, Nicki."

She shrugged. "I do what I must. It is the Greek way."

"How did you get so banged up?"

"I fall down some steps in Thera. I run through some backyards and get cut by branches. Here," she said, sticking a finger through a hole in her black jeans, "is where a dog bit me."

"And your lip?"

"They roughed me up a bit. Not much. I know when to play the dead dog."

"Not a fun night on the town, ma'am. Want to put something on those cuts while I dress? I have some first aid cream in the bathroom."

Wincing in pain, she wagged her head. Then she realized that Cassie might want some privacy to change her clothes. "Yes. Yes, I do."

When Nicki returned from the bathroom, Cassie was draping a navy sweater around her shoulders. The evening was warm, but the wind would be cool in Athinios.

"Hurry, Britt," Nicki said, her fingers tapping on the desk.

Suddenly, a loud knock rattled the hallway door. Cassie and Nicki's eyes locked, the thought flashing through each mind that Britt had returned. It couldn't be, though. She would have come back through the outside doors.

The knocks sounded again, this time more urgent. "Britt? Cassie? Are you there?"

"It's Bob!" Cassie cried in a loud whisper. "It's okay," she assured Nicki as she pulled open the door, "I used to go out with him."

"Hiya!" Collins said, nonchalantly striding into the room. He stopped to take in the scene before him. "Well, well, well, my young lady, has Ms. Burkhardt had her way with you, too?"

"Bob, cut it out," Cassie said. "This is a friend of Britt's. Nicki. From Athens."

"Where's Britt?" he asked Cassie, now ignoring Nicki. "Why?"

"That's my business. Where is she?"

Cassie gripped the cuffs of the sweater hanging around her neck and looped the arms around each other. Britt had suspected Bob of being involved with Bounty's death. Could she have been right? The programmer tightened the knot in her sweater so that the arms hung like thick ribbons over her chest. "In Thera. She's having dinner with Dr. Gavas."

"Now, why don't I believe you? How about you, Nicki, you know where she is?"

The Greek shook her head. "I check at her pension. They say to come here. I come here."

"No Britt. How about that?" Collins unzipped his jacket. The handle of his automatic popped out. "Well, gang, let's go find her."

"Where the hell are they?" Britt muttered as she trotted down the corridor from Cassie's room. Maybe, she thought, they had decided to wait in the car. But there the brown Golf sat, parked alongside the courtyard curb, looking garish under a string of bare, white bulbs.

"Maria," Britt said, returning to the front desk, "did you see Cassie leave?"

The widow lifted her fingers from a square calculator set next to an open ledger. Her eyebrows rose in sympathy. "Ah, you just missed her. She left two, three minutes ago with Bob and a young lady."

"Bob! Are you sure?"

"Yes, of course. Why should I mistake such a thing?"

"You wouldn't, Maria," Britt said. Panic rose like heated mercury from her stomach to her throat. "Did they say where they were going?"

Maria shook her head. "No. They drove away in Bob's car."

"What was he driving?"

"A Mercedes. His usual car."

"Thanks," Britt cried over her shoulder as she ran back to Cassie's room. Dumping the contents of her lover's purse on the bed, her shaky fingers snatched the car keys out of the pile.

"Where am I going?" she said to herself as she started up the Golf. Not to the beach. They would have walked, not driven there. Maybe Nicki became anxious and persuaded Bob to drive them to Athinios. But why would Cassie go with them? No, it was all terribly wrong.

As she pulled out of the courtyard, a Nissan driving by the entrance screeched to a halt. By the time Britt had gained the main road into Kamari, the car had turned around. It closed in behind her, its bright lights bearing down on her.

She speeded through Kamari proper, then twisted through the curves outside town, heading inland. She passed the Fira Winery, dark and lifeless on the inland plain.

Past the curve leading to Exo Geno, Britt opened up the throttle. The Japanese model stayed with her, blinking its lights. Then, when it was nearly on her bumper, the driver flipped on the interior light. In her rearview mirror, Britt saw Rich Marcello frantically motioning for her to pull over. She nearly drove into a tomato field doing so.

"What the hell is going on!" she cried, running to Marcello's car.

"Jump in. I'll explain."

She slid into the passenger's seat next to the embassy official.

"Fancy driving, lady. You okay?" Marcello said as Britt closed the door.

"No. I'm on the verge of panic."

Marcello switched off the headlights. The black Mediterranean night filled the car.

"Cassie's gone," Britt said. She pressed her lips together to keep them from quivering. "She left with Bob Collins and Nicki."

"Slow down and start from the beginning."

Quickly Britt provided the details of Nicki's appearance, her story of the smuggling, and of their plan to drive Nicki to Athinios. "But I don't know what happened. Bob showed up and they took off."

Marcello picked up a portable radio next to him. "Just a sec." He slid the antenna out the car window. "Alex? Alex?" he called.

"Here, my friend," came the reply, choppy with static.

"I have Britt."

"Good. Where's Nicki?"

"Collins has her. Also Cassie Burkhardt. We're going after them now. I'll be in touch."

"Who are you talking to?" Britt asked.

"Alexander Stamos. An investigator pal of mine from Athens. He went to Thera to find out what busted the phone system. Someone torched the whole damn building. Probably with gasoline and a handful of grenades." Marcello snapped the antenna in place on the hand-held unit, then tossed it in the back seat.

Marcello glanced at Britt, then stared into the darkness. "As far as what's going on..." He told her what had been in the report from Washington, that the real Robert Collins had been dead for nine years.

"But if that's not Bob, who is he?" she whispered.

"A cockroach. We haven't fixed the name yet."

"But he has Cass...and Nicki...we've got to find them!"

"You know this island. Where do we start?"

"This can't be happening," Britt said, gripping the dash.

"Take three deep breaths, then think, professor. I need your brain functioning now, not your emotions."

Britt sucked in the cooling night air, focusing her thoughts.

"Now, where would they be?" Marcello asked.

"Okay. I see three good possibilities: the *Praxis*, the winery, or the airport."

"Count the *Praxis* out. She's in the Thera harbor. Alex has her covered. He'll contact us if anyone tries to board."

"That leaves the winery and the airport," Britt said. "Probably not at the winery. It looked shut down when we passed it. I'd say they're at the airport."

"Going with the cargo. Makes sense." Marcello checked his watch. "I lay money on the airport, too. Get them off the island ASAP—"

"He won't hurt them, will he?"

"You know the answer to that one. It's the two of us, Britt. We stop Collins and his buddies now or we don't stop them at all. We won't have a second chance."

"We stop them at the airport," Britt said, "and I know how to do it."

25

Alexander Stamos leaned on a low stone wall and faced the western sea, his eyes fastened on the *Praxis* far below him. On the ledge, next to his elbow, sat the radio unit that kept him in contact with Rich Marcello. Behind him the shadows outlined the narrow doorway of a shuttered home in Thera. Above him, sounds of the carefree night life drifted down from tavernas embedded in the cliffs—the wailing melodies of Middle–Eastern music and the rise and fall of conversation and laughter.

The breeze rushing across the sea–filled crater whipped up the cliffs with a gale force. Stamos zipped his windbreaker all the way to his throat. "You fool," he muttered to himself as he thought of the warm sweaters folded in the dresser drawers of his Athens apartment. He knew the islands better, how the hot June days could turn into cool nights on Santorini.

Stamos dug his knuckles into his eyes and let his pair of compact Nikon binoculars bounce against his rib cage. No one had boarded the yacht the entire time he had been watching. He reached under his jacket for a package of Cleopatras, his eyes never leaving the luxury yacht of the Alevras family. He tapped the small box against his free hand. A couple of cigarettes jockeyed into view. Just as Stamos selected his smoke, an arm swung across the door frame and grabbed his windbreaker, then jerked the investigator onto the narrow path with a head–snapping motion.

The Greek fended off a blow with his forearm, but the next swing caught his solar plexus. As Stamos sank to the ground, the assailant knocked the radio unit from the ledge and sent it clattering down the cliff. Then Stamos felt a heavy blow at the back of his neck. He crumpled to the ground, clutching at the cobblestones. He rolled to his side, awake but not alert, and did not move.

A man's laugh and a woman's flirtatious lilt sounded nearby. Stamos wanted to cry for help, but he had no breath for words. The couple's presence proved help enough. The attacker withdrew, striding swiftly down the twisted path and disappearing into the night.

Stamos cracked open an eye. Sandals and rows of wiggling toes lined up next to his nose. "Arghhh," he said. "Hawww."

He heard *Disgusting drunk!* in an ethereal voice, floating high above him. The world went soft and out of focus as the investigator wheezed in a tiny bit of air.

"I thought we were going to Thera," Cassie said.

"Changed my mind." Collins adjusted the rearview mirror so he could have a better view of Nicki in the back seat. In the time they had been on the road, no one had approached him from behind.

"What about Britt? I thought you wanted her."

"I'll leave her for others."

"To do what?"

"Probably what I'd do," Collins said, giving Cassie a cockeyed grin. "Get her in the sand and show her what real sex is like, then dump her about twenty miles out at sea."

"You bastard!" Cassie cried, lunging at Collins across the front seat.

Collins blocked her punch with his arm, then shoved Cassie into the passenger door. "You stay there, or I'll blow your friend's brains out the back window."

"I don't care!" Cassie swung a right hook at him. It glanced off his shoulder.

Collins hit the brakes, sending Cassie into the dashboard. Her forearm banged into a row of radio knobs on the dash, leaving a jagged tear that quickly swelled with blood.

Nicki, propelled forward, grabbed at Collins's throat. But Collins already had his automatic out, and he thrust the barrel into the side of Nicki's head. The steel glanced off the architect's cranium. Nicki flopped back into her seat, moaning.

"Christ," Cassie said, trying to staunch her inch–long cut.

"There may be a towel in the glove compartment," Collins said, stepping back on the gas. "I don't want you bleeding all over these seats."

"What the hell do you care? Why don't you just kill us now?"

"I've got a few plans for you."

"We're going to the airport, aren't we?" Cassie said. She found a square of linen and used it to apply pressure to the wound. "Why?"

"You'll find out." Collins caught Nicki shifting slightly toward the car door. A river of blood ran over her ear and branched onto her cheek. "Hey, stupid, one of you escapes, the other dies. Now plug up your goddamn head. I don't want you to spoil my car with your blood!"

Nicki eased herself back into position in the middle of the Mercedes' seat. She pressed the sleeve of her sweatshirt against her head, but out of spite made sure several drops of blood spotted the leather cushions.

"You know, Nicki, you remind me of Bounty," Collins said. "Remember him, Cass? I gave him his last ride. Try to be smarter than he was, you guys."

For Cassie, all sound faded from the car. Even the engine seemed to go silent. "Did you kill him?" she asked.

A wide grin spread across Collins's face. "I'd say Bounty killed himself. I just helped him along."

"You would not tell us this," Nicki said weakly, "unless you plan to kill us." She checked the stain on her shirt. The flow seemed to have diminished.

"You know," Collins said, fixing his attention on the road, "none of this would be happening if Britt hadn't have been so damn clever in Athens. I nearly ran her down in the Plaka. She could have just been in the hospital. Now she's going to be dead." The lights of the airport glowed like an interment camp a short way up the road.

"You were the one in the truck?" Nicki asked.

"You get the prize, little lady," Collins said as the car rolled to a stop by the terminal.

"I hope so," Nicki said, her eyes catching Cassie's. With that, the Greek jerked on the car handle and leapt from the car. But she had underestimated her weakness. Her knees buckled before she had taken three steps. As she lay on the ground, trying to push herself upright, Collins snapped the gun into her head one more time. Nicki slumped to the dust, unconscious.

Britt swerved Cassie's car into the dark alley next to the motor scooter rental shop at Kamari Beach. Through the open back door of the Pelican Taverna next door, she heard music and the sharp chatter of cooks and waiters. The aroma of roasted lamb seeped into the night.

She picked up a five–liter fuel can from a haphazard row of containers at the rear of the shop. Setting the can next to the single fuel pump, Britt tried to lift the nozzle out of its position. A short chain, looped through the handle and fixed with a padlock, stopped her. She yanked at the links a couple of times. They held fast.

"Damn." She hustled to the twenty mopeds and scooters lined along the alleyway. Another chain ran through the spokes of the rear wheels of all the two–wheelers, securing them together. Britt unscrewed the cap of the fuel tank of the first moped. The tank was nearly full.

After replacing the cap, Britt pulled the chain taunt, so that a yard of extra chain lay at her feet. Then she carefully tipped the Girabaldi on its side and positioned the fuel can under the mouth of the tank. Slowly, she unscrewed the cap. Gasoline poured out of the tank, most running into the can, but a bit spilling to the ground.

When the flow changed from a steady gush to a dribble, Britt righted the moped and replaced the cap. She rubbed her nose against the irritating fumes, then ran to the other end of the line, and repeated the operation with the last vehicle on that end. Just as she twisted the cap on the fuel can, the back door of the taverna creaked open.

A rush of Greek exploded into the night.

Britt rose to her full height. "Andreas," she said, addressing the owner of the Pelican, "it's me—Britt. I need gas for my moped. We ran out. Cassie stayed with the Vespa." Britt pointed up the road.

Andreas wiped his hands on the white towel tied around his hips. "You run out of petrol?"

Britt nodded. She pointed at the pump. "It was locked."

"Cassie, she is far away?"

"A few miles. I'm going to take the gas in the car. She's waiting so I have to go." Britt reached into her fanny pack and withdrew several bills. "Here," she said, pressing five hundred drachmas into Andreas's palm, "give this to the owner tomorrow, or whoever is on duty here. It should pay for what I'm taking. I'll bring the can back some other time."

Andreas held up his hands. "No, no. You give them the money yourself."

"Andreas, please. I'm not sure if I'll be here tomorrow."

Reluctantly, the taverna owner accepted the blue and white bills. Britt turned back to the task at hand.

"You will be all right?"

"Fine," Britt replied, giving the cap on the can an extra twist. She picked up the plastic container and loaded it in Cassie's Golf. Andreas watched her, the money in his hand, then retreated to his building shaking his head.

As soon as he had disappeared, Britt lifted the fuel can from the car and stashed it in the alley. No need to take it, when she'd be back this way again.

"You don't need to bring Britt into this. You have us. That should be enough." Cassie dabbed at the cut in her arm. A few beads of blood swelled to the surface. Nicki was sprawled next to her on the floor of the airport terminal, still unconscious. Cassie had torn off a strip of her shirt and tied it around the architect's head. Two small stains dotted the cloth.

Collins, who had been examining a time table with Theo Alevras, looked up. "You don't get it, do you?" he said. "I'm too close to let anyone stop me, even you and your honey pot. By daybreak, I'll be set up for life."

"Just what are you selling?"

"Some very fine goods. That's all you need to know."

"Where's the Bob I used to know?"

"Don't get sentimental, babe. You know, I've been grubbing around this stretch of sea for two years waiting for this break. I've set up my network. Now I'm ready to go legit. No more back door deals trying to protect the identities of one political party or another. No more kissing the butts of lackeys to dictators. After this delivery, they'll be licking my rump to cut deals. Tonight I prove I can deliver the goods."

"We prove, partner," Alevras said.

"Right," Collins replied.

Alevras headed for the door and made kissy expressions at Cassie as he whisked by. He gave Collins a long look of appraisal before he stepped through the doorway. Cassie caught the look of distrust in his eyes.

"Arms, I take it," she said. "It's a pretty competitive market, from what I hear."

"Not so with specialty items. Whatever is needed, I can do it and be legitimate about it, too. Mediterranean Technologies, Inc. That's the name of my company. I'll be able to retire when I'm forty and spend the rest of my life cruising and partying. Maybe even dig up a few of your precious pots. I've developed an appreciation for archaeology, if you can believe it."

"Bullshit." Cassie ran her eyes across the half dozen guards milling in the office. One lazily bobbed an AK–47 in her direction. *You plan to kill us*, Nicki had said. Cassie moved to a straight back chair and lowered herself carefully, her hands in front of her. As the soldier's weapon tracked her movement, Cassie felt the cold hollow of truth spread out from her diaphragm. Nicki had been right.

Stamos fought a rising nausea. He didn't want to sit up just yet. He took three shallow breaths, then three deep ones and eased himself upright. His communication device was gone. Over the edge, he remembered. His binoculars bumped against his chest.

The Greek pulled himself to his feet, using the low retaining wall in front of him as support. He peered down into the harbor.

The *Praxis* was gone! The Santorini wind slapped him into comprehension. But wait. The yacht heaved in the distance, approaching the northern tip of the island. Stamos sank back to the ground, his legs feeling like rubber bands. He had no way to contact Rich Marcello. He had no way to warn him.

He struggled to his feet. He knew where Marcello would be. Now he had to get there!

26

"All I need is luck and a bungee cord," Britt muttered as she stepped into the cool night air off her patio. She shut the French doors softly behind her and snapped the door lock into place. Inside her wetsuit, a book of matches wrapped in plastic, stuck to her like a medical patch.

As she turned to step on the path alongside the pension, an arm enveloped her head and a moist hand clamped over her mouth.

"You be quiet," a rough voice ordered in a thick accent.

Britt tried to slip the vice–like hold by letting her body go limp. The man quickly hoisted her by the waist and carted her under his meaty arm like an oversized child. With her arms pinned, Britt kicked the air without finding a target.

For a moment, Britt thought she would pass out, she could get so little air through her nose. What air she got had a sour fish odor. Nicki's story of her attackers aboard the ferry flashed through her mind. One of them, she had said, was as squat as a shrine and stunk like a fisherman.

Anton Vrouvas cut through the pistachio grove with his prize to the darkened road leading into Kamari. The distance was short—only thirty yards or so—but the danger of discovery was grave with rooms of tourists within shouting distance. He tightened his hand over Britt's mouth.

As they approached a dark Volvo, Britt saw a figure in the front seat lean over and snap open the back door. The professor kicked with more fury, knowing she had to break away now. It would be her only chance. Once they got her in the car, they could take her anywhere and do anything.

When Vrouvas swung Britt toward the gaping hole, he was so intent on keeping her mouth covered, that his arm slipped a little way toward her chest. Britt rolled her hips under and brought her legs up in a half–tuck. Vrouvas grunted as the shifting weight threatened his grip. Feeling herself slip further through his arm, Britt thrust her legs forward and caught the edge of the door frame with her rubber–soled shoes. Using all the force of her legs, she pushed against the car, straining back against her captor and twisting like a snagged tarpon. His sweaty hand slid off her mouth. Instead of shouting for help, Britt bit the smelly flesh as hard as she could. The Greek cried out in pain. Quickly, Britt brought the heel of her foot back into his groin. He yelped and doubled over, letting go of the professor. Britt tumbled to the ground. By the time Vrouvas's companion, Dios Genoulis, had opened the driver's door, Britt had gained her feet and started back toward her room, running with a jerky motion at first as her legs adjusted to the adrenalin pumping through her.

As she rounded a corner of the pension, a hunk of plaster exploded. The smack of the bullet had been much louder than the dying ping of the gun's report. Britt had seen enough movies to know he was using a silencer.

She sped along the concrete sidewalk to the front of the pension where her Vespa was parked. She ripped the two bungee cords off the back of the scooter in passing, then broke into a wild run through the small squares of grape fields. She cut to the north to take advantage of a stretch of pistachio trees, their scrawny trunks and branches providing slim coverage. She would take what she could get, though. She heard two shots zip through the leaves behind her. A cluster of nuts thudded to the ground.

Passing a brightly lit pension, Britt fought the impulse to run inside and cry for help. But she knew explanations would take time, and that was a luxury that could cost the lives of Cassie and Nicki.

Instead, Britt followed the curve of the grove to the southeast, which brought her closer to the beach. She glanced back and saw her pursuer laboring through the fields, following her tracks. When Dios Genoulis saw her veer to the south, though, he cut diagonally across a quarter acre patch of tomatoes, narrowing the distance substantially. As Britt ran past the framework of the partially constructed pension off the main road into Kamari, she swung quickly around a corner and darted through an open doorway. In the dark interior, she could make out only the doorways and windows illuminated by pale moonlight. Squatting, she patted the dirt floor, searching for a weapon. She found nothing.

"Think! Think!" she ordered. What had she seen before, before the walls of the building had been set into place? The night she and Cassie strolled home talking of love, the night Cassie invited her in and...yes, she remembered one of the workers securing a plank across a stairwell. It would have been on the west side of the house. Britt made her way through a door. At the side of what would someday be the kitchen, she discovered the plank, and an unfinished stairwell going to a lower level. She picked up the short two–by–eight and waited.

As the seconds passed, Britt fought a desire to shriek, "Come here you bastard!" An electric current pulsated through her muscles, and the veins in her arms bulged.

Then Britt heard her assailant's footsteps crunch the hard, dry soil nearby. She ran her tongue over her lips. Quietly, she sidled over to the open doorway and waited for him to pass. She heard nothing. Even the wind died to an oppressive silence. For a moment, Britt doubted her senses. Had her hearing failed? She peeked furtively around the unfinished structure, through the gaping holes where windows and doors would be hammered into place. He was nowhere to be heard, nowhere to be seen.

Suddenly, he appeared, stalking along the wall in the next room. Britt pressed herself into the shadows behind the open doorway. She tried to listen for the intruder scraping along the floor, but the wind had risen again and whistled loudly through the structure.

Then his outline appeared in the door. Carefully, the Greek stepped through the opening, breathing heavily. Britt held her breath. The man advanced a yard to his right. He thrust out his gun with one hand. With the other, he mopped his brow with the sleeve of his jacket. *One more step*, Britt commanded, *take one more step.*

It came as a small step, more of a half–shuffle, but it was enough. Britt leapt toward him and rammed the plank into the back of his knees. He grasped at the walls for his balance, then toppled headlong down the steps. Panting, Britt waited for half a beat, then dropped the plank. She dashed for the beach, the bungee cords twisting in her hands like snakes.

Rich Marcello rolled to a stop at the hurricane fence outside the airport. A guard rested his broad back against the closed gate and blew smoke rings toward the Big Dipper. Marcello left his lights on, purposely blinding the defender.

"Hey, buddy!" he cried, leaning out the driver's window. "Let me past!"

The young man threw down the cigarette and ambled toward the car. Dressed in a green camouflage uniform and hightop sneakers, he stopped next to the driver's window. "You American?"

"You bet. I gotta get in to see Collins. Bob Collins."

The guard's face stiffened a bit. His black eyes examined the stranger. "Collins? What do you want?"

"You deaf? I want Collins. He told me to meet him out here."

"He says nothing to me. I am to let no one through."

"If you don't let me through, Collins will snap your head off like a pop top. I'll see to it personally."

"You have business with him?"

"I am his business. That's my stuff he's shipping to Cyprus. I bought it. Got it, amigo? Why don't you call him on your radio? If you know how to work it."

The muscles on the guard's face bulged. "You wait. I call," he said, unfastening the radio unit from his belt."

"You do that," Marcello said, surreptitiously flicking on the channels to his own unit.

The guard's radio squealed with static. The young man played with a few tuning knobs, then shrugged. "It is broke."

"Then hop in and ride with me to the terminal. You can tell Collins you're my escort. I'll tell him to get his goons some decent equipment."

"You turn off the car first," the guard ordered.

Marcello clicked off the ignition. The guard unlocked the gate and swung the wide steel barrier open. "Okay," the guard said, slipping into the back seat, his Uzi pointed at Marcello's head, "we go to the terminal."

"Now you're talking, buddy," Marcello said, checking his watch and suppressing a smile. Britt should be on her way now.

The night winds swept over the blackened sea, chopping it into a field of glittering shards, reflecting the light from the thick wedge of moon overhead. The strong wind meant a quick trip. Britt lowered Cassie's sailboard into the water. She strapped the can of gas that she had retrieved from the rental shop to the second aft footstrap. Before lifting herself onto the board, she stood for a few moments knee–deep in the cold water gathering her concentration.

The surf lapped at her legs while Britt marveled at Homer's wine–dark sea and the black sky filled with hard points of light. Once the Minoans had stood on this very beach looking into a night such as this. The Trojans had stood on their shores, the Greeks on theirs. Above all of them, the constellations of their destiny rotated. Life was theirs to seize by merely stepping forward, by accepting the wonder and the risk, the gain and the loss.

"Athena," Britt said aloud, "you'd better be with me on this one."

She tucked her hair into the hood of her wetsuit, then placed a knee on the sailboard. In one swift, strong motion, she swung herself upright. Water ran off the dark synthetic fabric. Beneath her, the board was as firm as the earth.

Her mind cleared. Britt knew what she had to do. She slid her feet, protected by reef shoes, into the middle footstraps. She pulled on the uphaul line. The sail rose out of the water and filled with the night winds. Britt gripped the boom and in moments was bouncing across the skin of the dark sea.

She concentrated on the bend of her knees, the straightness of her back. It had to be a perfect run; a spill would waste valuable time. She was behind schedule already.

As the wind gathered strength, Britt moved both feet behind the mast base. Her grip on the boom was firm and confident. In minutes she reached the promontory separating Kamari Beach from the airport, and separating her from Cassie. Cassie was on the other side, wasn't she? She'd have to be.

Britt felt Cassie's presence as she rounded the nub of land and saw the brilliant lights of the airstrip burst through the darkness. A plane was on the runway, a truck pulled alongside. Five men—probably workers from the winery—were loading crates.

Instead of moving inland, Britt steered out to sea, not wanting to be spotted by the crew. If she landed to the north of them, she figured she would be safe, with the coast hidden by an outcropping of land. Cold sea spray splashed her from head to foot. The air, smelling of salt, was crisp and invigorating. The perfect combination of wind, wave, and muscle, propelled her across the black water.

Just as she felt at the height of her power, she saw something that made her heart nearly explode: the *Praxis* cutting around the northern bend bearing straight for her.

27

Marcello swung open the wood frame door of the airport terminal, his pimply–faced escort three steps to the rear. The ticket counter was deserted, as were the orange plastic chairs arranged in rows in the middle of the room. Behind the counter, the second hand of a large industrial clock stuttered around the dial.

After a day's worth of near–tropic sun, the building had become an oven. With one hand Marcello loosened his tie and unbuttoned his collar. It was almost midnight. Britt should be at the airport by now. Where was she?

Someone in a black T–shirt and blue jeans popped out of a door in the back. The guard at Marcello's side let loose with a flurry of explanation in Greek.

"Shut up," Marcello boomed. "I'm from the U.S. Embassy in Athens. Who's in authority here?"

"I am. What is it that you want?"

"Who are you?" Marcello thundered. Based on Britt's description of Theo Alevras, Marcello assumed it was he.

"I ask the questions here. You say you are from the Embassy?"

"That's right. I've been told that you're holding an American woman hostage here. A Cassandra Burkhardt."

"Your information is wrong. No hostages here. This is a military airport. You go now. We are closed."

"Military, eh? Then where are the soldiers?"

Alevras grinned. "They are on leave this evening. The commanding officer is a friend of mine."

Marcello glanced around the room. It was lifeless, with a couple of travel posters hanging on the dirty mint–green walls to give it color. Flies and the overhead lights buzzed in harmony. If Nicki and Cassie were here, Marcello thought, they'd have to be in one of the back rooms. Most likely the room from which Alevras had just emerged.

Marcello made a quick appraisal of Theo Alevras, son of Dimitris. "The situation is unacceptable. I demand recourse."

Alevras screwed up his face at the words he hadn't learned in school, or from his English speaking girlfriends. His pride, though, forbade him from asking for an explanation. "This man of mine," he said, gesturing to the youth who had accompanied Marcello from the front gate, "will escort you from the grounds. Please go. We do not want to hurt you."

"All right. All right, I'll go." Marcello's voice was loud, angry. "But I'll be back in the morning with government officials."

"Noooo!" The cry he had hoped to hear sliced through the terminal. A woman's voice. Cassie's, he was sure.

Marcello and Alevras froze for a moment, their eyes locked. The cry had torn the veil from the masquerade.

The guard stepped back from Marcello and lowered his Uzi as Alevras yelled for help from the rear office. Moving on instinct, Marcello whirled around and knocked the guard's weapon to the side, then jumped over a row of chairs just as the back room door swung open. As two machine gun barrels protruded from the doorway, Marcello drew the hand gun tucked at the small of his back.

"Sorry, kid," he said, as he shot the startled guard in the chest. He then snapped around and fired one round into the door jamb. As the weapons withdrew, he angled himself to make a dash for the front door. But another guard filled the passage, his AK–47 cradled to shoot. Marcello wheeled around, desperate. His only choice was to take cover behind the ticket counter. He fired at the front door, then leaped over the high block of wood, crashed into the wall behind it, and landed on the linoleum on all fours.

The room vibrated in silence, like the shocked moment after an earthquake. Crouching, Marcello listened for Britt's arrival. Still no sound from the airstrip. What the hell had happened to her? Now he was trapped. He heard a rush of Greek, then silence.

After conversing with Alevras, a guard plucked a grenade from his vest. A small click sounded as he pulled the pin from its mooring. Gripping the explosive tightly, the guard aimed for Marcello's hiding place. Just as he was about to lob the metal ball, Alexander Stamos burst through the doors and shot him. Seconds later, the grenade exploded.

Britt cut due west to avoid the rapidly approaching yacht. She leaned into the sharp turn and felt the surf surge near her backside. Only seconds from shore, she knew she had to concentrate on her approach, not on the deep–throated yells floating over the sea from the *Praxis*.

She heard a series of whining reports, and two holes burst through the orange sail. Britt heaved the sail around, then dropped it into the water as the board scraped into the stones on the beach. In a moment, a boat filled with armed men came screaming across the water from the yacht.

Britt quickly released the bungee cords that bound the gas can to the footstraps. She scrambled behind the small monastery at the northeastern corner of the airstrip. Placing her back against the cool, whitewashed surface, she tried to catch her breath.

She peeked from behind the structure. A Cessna Citation sat nearly fifty yards away, facing south, ready for take–off. Now, only a couple of workers loaded crates on the plane from a pickup nestled near the left wing. Another fifty yards away, the terminal glowed in the bright lights of the airstrip.

Britt glanced at her watch. Damn. She was ten minutes late. She had to move now and hope that Marcello was already at the terminal. And hope that the men from the *Praxis* would not find her within their sights. Suddenly, she heard a pop across the airfield, then several more. Gunfire. Then a small explosion. The men at the plane shouted to one another. Stretching out for a look, she saw them gallop across the tarmac toward the terminal. Now was her time to act.

Taking a deep breath, she dashed to the twin engine jet. Leaving the gas can on the ground, she stuck her head through the doorway. Rows of crates on palates lined the fuselage, which had been stripped of passenger seats. She called for Cassie and Nicki. No one answered. The plane was deserted.

Britt grabbed the plastic container of fuel and doused the tires with the gas. Dark rivers stained the concrete, and the biting odor of petroleum permeated the air. She poured a trail to the open door, then tossed the nearly empty can into the plane. Steady, now, steady, she told herself, drawing the box of matches from inside her wet suit. The first strike broke the match. The second strike lit and held. She tossed the tiny flame on the left tire. With a whooshing sound, it burst into a glorious and dangerous blaze. The fire rolled across the tarmac to the right wheel and engulfed it, then leapt into the interior of the craft. Britt felt the intense heat through her wetsuit as she turned back toward the tiny monastery and began to run. She peeled off the confining hood and let her hair spill out.

Before she had taken more than a few steps, she saw that the men from the *Praxis,* led by her old acquaintance Artemios, had gained the beach. He and another man were scurrying across the tarmac to head her off. Two others, their feet planted in the sand, gaped at the burning plane, while a couple more were running back to their boat. For Britt, retreat behind the monastery was impossible now. She had only one place to go.

Britt spun around and raced toward the terminal. Just as she reached the side of the building, the plane exploded behind her. Instinctively, Britt dove to the brick–hard ground to blunt the impact of the explosion on her. As the shock wave swept across the open land, Britt lay still, her heart pumping with adrenaline, ready for her next move.

As horrible as the explosion was on the ground, from a small plane overhead it looked like the ruin of all joy to Mikos Zerakis. The Greek official prayed to all the powers of the Trinity that no one had been hurt, especially his goddaughter Nicki. Nor those poor American girls. No one deserved a death by fire, except the Nazis and the bastards of the junta.

"We will have to land," he told the officer next to him. "Set the wheels down on the southern edge of the airstrip, put the brakes on hard. We do not need much room to stop." The officer did not reply, aware that Zerakis spoke from emotion, not knowledge of aviation.

Zerakis had only a dozen soldiers on board, but they were a special tactical team pried from the Army. He had had to call the President for them, who first refused, then agreed when Zerakis threatened to share with the press not only the name of the President's mistress, but certain photographs that had fallen into his hands last winter. Zerakis grimaced. He had traded much for the President's help, revealing information that could have been put to better use at another time, and he had done it all based on the intelligence from the Criminal Investigative Services and the U.S. Embassy. If the life of his favorite goddaughter had not been at stake, he would never have gotten involved. Politics being what they were, if C.I.S. and that Marcello fellow had been wrong, the President would have ruined him over this episode. But they were right. The evidence lay burning below him.

The pilot circled once, closely observing the southern end of the runway. On the next pass, he set down the government's Beechcraft 1900, painted with the white and blue of the Greek flag. He taxied the turboprop as close to the terminal as he dared. Before the wheels stopped, the doors flew open and twelve heavily armed men leaped to the tarmac. The politician waited inside until the area was secure.

Staring dumbfounded through the now shattered window facing the airstrip, Theo Alevras repeated "the plane is gone" for the tenth time. Nearly catatonic, he noticed neither the blood streaming down the side of his face from a small cut above his temple, nor the panic of the guards behind him. The small pops from the gun battle out front, where Marcello and Stamos continued to fight with his followers, held no interest for him.

As he watched, an airplane rolled into view. It turned toward the terminal and slowly moved across the hot, cracked field, carefully avoiding the chunks of smoldering debris littering the ground. The plane parked a short distance from the terminal, its door facing away from the building.

"Papa?" Alevras said. "Papa, please be you."

Cassie turned from the fiery scene out the window. "It's over, Bob," she said. "There's no way off this island."

"We've got the *Praxis*!" Collins shouted. "Get moving, Theo!"

Alevras slowly wheeled around, his jaw slack, his eyes glazed. "We? I have the *Praxis*, you mean."

"I'm not going with you," Cassie said.

"Think again!" Bob cried, waving his Beretta at her.

"Never! You kill me now or you let me go."

"My pleasure," he said, raising the automatic to fire. "Then, Theo, it's your turn."

Britt watched the plane blaze in the distance. Sitting upright now, she wiped dust from her eyes with dirty hands. With her ears still ringing from the explosion, she heard muffled shouts coming from within the building.

Britt scrambled to her feet, then carefully crept next to the whitewashed wall, glowing yellow from the raging fire in the distance. Slowly, she leaned her head toward the open side window. The sight nearly made her knees buckle: Collins in a rage, brandishing an automatic under Cassie's nose.

Britt grabbed for the closest projectile in sight—a chunk of lava rock about the size of a baseball. Gripping the stone with all fingers, the professor eyeballed her target and went into a quick wind up. Just as Bob moved the automatic in Theo's direction, she released the rock and watched it sail toward its target.

The black chunk hurtled through the side window and struck Collins in the middle of the back. His gun clattered to the floor and fired, slicing off the top of his Reebok. Blood flowed from a mangle of bone and flesh.

Cassie grabbed the automatic and held it between the palms of her hands, still tied at the wrist. She pointed the Beretta at Alevras, who backed away in disbelief.

"Do something! Do something!" the Greek playboy yelled at his men, now crouching helplessly, frozen in shock.

Britt dove through the window head–first as Collins, screaming in pain, reached for Theo's gun with one hand while trying to stop the flow of blood with the other. Britt kicked the gun out of his reach.

The door splintered open and a soldier in a black beret yelled for surrender, his backup just steps behind. The smugglers quickly dropped their weapons on the floor.

In moments, grunts and sobs filled the room, as did the smell of sweat, blood, and gunpowder. Zerakis's men snatched the firearms away from the captives and kicked the enemy into spread–eagle positions on the floor. One soldier, crouching in a thickening pool of blood, tended to Collins. A haunting quiet momentarily descended on the scene, then was replaced by the piercing barks from the commanding officer, striding into the room to take charge.

Zerakis marched into the room behind him.

"Good to see you, Mikos," Britt said, springing forward.

"And you, my friend. You are not hurt?"

"I'm fine."

"Where is Nicki?"

Britt looked to Cassie, her arms stiff in front of her as a soldier cut the rope around her wrists.

"Over here." Cassie nodded toward a corner of the room. Rubbing her sore wrists, she explained. "They beat her."

"But I live," Nicki called out, rising unsteadily on her hands. "I play the dead dog again. Perhaps that is my destiny, eh, professor?"

Zerakis called out to a soldier, who scurried over with a first aid kit. "You fix her," he ordered, "then she goes on the jet back to Athens. Hurry."

"Mr. Zerakis?"

The member of Parliament turned to face a man in a dusty business suit.

"I'm Richard Marcello from the U.S. Embassy."

"Ah, yes. We meet at last."

"This is Alexander Stamos," Marcello said, motioning toward his companion. Their brief nod revealed their acquaintance.

"Come on, Cass," Britt said, taking her friend's elbow, "let's go outside and leave this mess to the pros." She mouthed a "we'll be back" to Nicki, who winked slowly, then gave herself over to medical inspection.

When they reached the door leading to the airstrip, Britt fingered Cassie's blood–soaked sleeve. "What happened here?"

"Tried to change the channel on the car radio the hard way." Cassie patted the wound gingerly. "It's okay. It stopped bleeding ages ago. I doubt I'll even need a stitch."

At first the night air was like a splash of water, cool and invigorating. Then came the smell of gasoline, burning rubber, and the ominous stench of melting synthetics. No attempt had been made to put out the flames of the burning plane.

"Are you okay otherwise?" Britt asked, ignoring the chaos.

"Now I am—except for the nightmares I'll have. I thought I was blowing into the Ultimate Wave. I would have been if..."

"It's over now." Britt pulled Cassie into her arms. The women's foreheads touched. "We're alive."

After a few moments, Cassie tilted back and inspected Britt. Her web of black hair held globs of sand, and smudges of soil linked themselves across her face like camouflage paint. "Am I as filthy as you are?" she said, brushing dirt from Britt's cheek.

"You're worse, I'm sure."

"Brat," Cassie said, catching a glint in Britt's eye and returning it.

"Come on," Britt smiled, "let's see Nicki off, then tell the boys we're splitting this party. Rich can meet us back at Kamari."

"How will we get there?" Cassie asked as they steered themselves toward the terminal.

"Your board's down on the beach. Ever ridden tandem?"

"No. I'm game, though," Cassie grinned.

"Uh, there are a couple of holes in the sail..."

"They won't stop us."

Britt tightened her grip on Cassie. "Babe, nothing ever will!"

28

"How was Nicki when you left?" Zerakis asked, signalling the American women to sit down in his Athens office. He took his place in his favorite office chair—a Queen Anne with burgundy leather. Rich Marcello resumed his seat after standing for the women's entrance.

"Fine," Britt grinned. "The nurses hover over her like a cooing baby."

"Good. She deserves such attention."

"Despite having two broken ribs and a nasty concussion, she's seems quite cheerful." Britt refrained from mentioning that Nicki was getting special attention filled with romantic possibilities from a nurse named Helen.

Mikos laughed. "Even better! She is a fighter, like her father says. Now we just need to find her a husband."

"I think a medal of bravery would be more appreciated," Britt suggested.

"Perhaps you are right," he said, giving the professor a knowing nod.

"What have you found out about Bob?" Cassie asked Marcello as the M.P. got up to fix them drinks.

"Our bloodhounds sniffed one garbage pit after another before we got a lock on him," Marcello said. "The guy's name is Arthur Henley. He's been a gofer for one of the biggest arms merchants in the Mediterranean and Middle East. Decided to go into business for himself."

"But there was a real Robert Collins," Britt said. "What's the connection?"

"College roommates. The genuine issue was a Classics student. Henley probably got the idea of posing as an archaeology student from him. Clever approach, using the various excavations around the Mediterranean as bases of operation. They gave him the perfect excuse for hopping from one troubled country to another, sewing up a network of arms buyers."

Zerakis handed Britt and Cassie each a gin and tonic.

"He came mighty close to succeeding," Marcello continued. "He had a great partner in Dimitris Alevras—ruthless, with his tentacles stretching into every major Mediterranean port." The embassy official accepted a freshened scotch and soda from the Greek patriarch.

"A man with a long reach," Zerakis said, reclaiming the Queen Anne, "but with a coward and fool for a son. Our police press Theo just a little," the Greek said, pinching together a thumb and forefinger, "and the boy cries for his mama."

"Yeah," Rich continued, "he blurted out enough to convict them all, and he's promised to testify in court. Even against his old man—who, by the way, was chowing on octopus at his club in Heraklion when all the action was going down. Too bad he didn't choke. Would have saved the trouble of a trial."

"What's going to happen to Collins—Henley?" Britt asked.

"He's up on a couple dozen charges, including the murder of Bountourakis. We're also trying to bust him on federal violations in the U.S. for illegal arms trading. Out of that mess at the airport, we've found pieces of measuring devices used in the production of chemical weapons and a bunch of triggers used for various types of bombs."

"They were going to Cyprus?" Britt asked.

"Actually, the plane was stopping there only for fuel and some additional cargo. It was scheduled to go on to a Middle East country—to this year's Number One dictator."

"But we stop them," Zerakis smiled, "and for that, we thank you."

"Couldn't have done it without you," Marcello said. "The 'unofficial' cooperation between our embassy and the Greek government won't be forgotten. At least not until the next political roosters get their tail feathers in a bunch."

Zerakis said nothing, but wore the thin, ambivalent smile of a true politician.

The following week, Cassie, Nicki, and her girlfriend Helen sat on the terrace of a taverna in Thera that clung precariously to the sides of the caldera cliffs. Waiting for Britt, they relaxed in the shade of a bright blue umbrella tipped to the southwest to protect them from the punishing afternoon sun.

"I'm glad you were able to come down for a few days," Cassie said. "You won't reconsider joining Britt and me on Crete?"

"No, we have reservations in Rhodes. It will be our honeymoon, eh?" Nicki winked at Helen, who smiled back shyly.

Like Nicki, Helen was petite, with short, black hair. Her face was a bit fuller, with a quick, warm smile. She took a sip of lemonade, then watched a small tourist tug nudge its nose into the pier on the largest volcanic island. "Your work here ends soon?" she asked. "Is that right?"

"Yep. Six more weeks."

"Will you be sorry to leave?"

"Not really. It's been fun, but it's time I got on with my life."

"What's next?"

"I'm seeing if my company has a job opening in Minnesota. If not," Cassie shrugged, "I'll find work with another company."

Britt and Jim Larson approached the table, their arms linked at the elbows.

"Well, here you are!" Cassie exclaimed, turning to them. "My, you two look pleased with yourselves."

Britt glanced at Jim. "We've just spent some time with Jim's future father–in–law. We had a good talk." She, Jim, and the Kazantas clan had agreed to let the little scam the family had been running become forgotten history.

Cassie patted Jim's arm. "Good for you!"

Britt took a sip from Cassie's half–full glass. "I'm sorry," Britt said, "but Cass and I have to run or we'll be late. Got our bags?"

"Over there, in the corner," Cassie replied, nodding in the direction of their two pieces sitting out of traffic's way.

"We'll say our good–byes here. No need for you to escort us."

"Good," said Nicki. "My body still creaks."

"Well, you're in the best hands possible," Britt said, giving her old friend a quick kiss on the cheek. "Take care of her, Helen, okay?"

The nurse grinned. "With pleasure. Nicki makes a very good patient."

After a round of hugs and kisses, Britt and Cassie broke away. "We'll see you in a couple of weeks in Athens. Have fun!"

"And do everything we're going to do!" Cassie cried. She turned to Britt with a playful smile, her blond hair holding a ring of light in the bright sun.

Nicki and Helen remained on the terrace after their friends and Jim left, sipping their drinks and finally ordering a light lunch. Half an hour later, and hundreds of feet below them, a ferry pulled away from the Thera harbor bound for Heraklion, Crete.

"There they go," Nicki said, pointing at the ship that appeared like a miniature model in a huge basin.

"You have good friends," Helen said, sliding her chair around for a better view.

"I'm lucky." She grasped Helen's hand. "In many ways."

"No," Helen touched a thin yellow streak under Nicki's eye, a remnant from a nasty bruise, "you were not so lucky this last time."

Nicki held Helen's hand to her cheek. "My injuries brought me to you. For that, I treasure each wound."

Helen pinched Nicki's arm playfully. "Do you love me more now?"

"If I did, I think I would pop." The godchild of Mikos Zerakis laughed with a full, happy voice. When Helen giggled, she laughed harder. It had been a long time since she had felt such pleasure. Suddenly, sitting with her love in a restaurant embedded in a cliff, watching a boat carry away two extraordinary friends, she felt happy. The gears of her life were meshing at last.

"They're on their way," Helen exclaimed, waving at the receding ferry. "Do you think they can see us?"

"Yes," Nicki replied thoughtfully. "I think they see everything."

Far below, Britt and Cassie stood at the stern of the ship, pressed against the railing. The cliffs of the caldera soared above them. "At last," Cassie said, "I have you alone."

Britt looked at the sunny deck strewn with students leaning against backpacks and sprawled on sleeping bags. "I don't consider this being alone, Cass."

"If I start kissing you, we would be. That should clear the deck."

"On the contrary, we'd draw such a crowd the boat would capsize. End over end."

"Let's risk it," Cassie said, pulling Britt close. The women kissed long and deep, as the salty wind swirled about them, and the chatter of excited voyagers and the sharp cries of circling gulls faded in the background.

Then they smiled at each other, shoulder to shoulder, leaning against the railing until the ship cleared the crater. Once in the open sea, they moved to the forward deck, where they could see their route, invisible on the dark waters of the Mediterranean to all but them.

Madwoman Press Titles

Lesbians in the Military Speak Out by Winni S. Webber
ISBN 0-9630822-3-X $9.95
Women from every branch of the armed forces tell their stories about being women and lesbians in the military.

Sinister Paradise by Becky Bohan
ISBN 0-9630822-2-1 $9.95
A professor of classics finds herself endangered by an international arms–smuggling conspiracy just as she finally finds love .

That's Ms. Bulldyke to You, Charlie! by Jane Caminos
ISBN 0-9630822-1-3 $8.95
Hilarious collection of single–panel cartoons that capture lesbian life in full. From dyke–teens and lipstick lesbians, to the highly-assimilated and the politically correct.

On the Road Again by Elizabeth Dean
ISBN 0-9630822-0-5 $9.95
Magazine columnist Ramsey Sears tours America, finding adventure and romance along the way.

You can buy Madwoman Press books at your local women's bookstore or order them directly from the publisher. Send direct orders to Madwoman Press, P.O.Box 690, Northboro, MA 01532. Please include $2.50 for shipping and handling of the first book ordered and $.50 for each additional book. Massachusetts residents please add 5% sales tax. A free catalog is available upon request.